"Rum," he repeated. "I must get away from here. Rum! Rum!"

I ran to fetch it, but my hands shook. I broke one glass and spilled a lot of rum. I heard a loud fall in the parlor. I ran in to find the captain lying full-length on the floor. At this point my mother, alarmed by the commotion, came running downstairs to help me. Between us we raised his head. He was breathing very loud and hard, but his eyes were closed and his face a horrible color.

We had no idea how to help the captain. . . . I got the rum and tried to put it down his throat, but his teeth were clamped tightly shut.

A Background Note about *Treasure Island*

The years 1650 to 1725 are sometimes called the Age of Piracy. In those years, large numbers of pirate ships roamed the oceans, attacking wealthy merchant ships and stealing their goods. Many of the ships the pirates attacked were carrying gold and silver from Central America to Europe. There were stories that some pirates buried huge treasures on uninhabited islands.

Although *Treasure Island* is not a true story, Stevenson uses these events as the background for his novel. He sets the story at some vague time shortly after the Age of Piracy. He imagines former pirates, now poor and with nothing to do, hanging around the dockside taverns in Bristol, England. They are desperate men who are anxious to get their hands on treasure that they feel they have a right to.

The story begins at an isolated inn on the rugged coast of England.

ROBERT LOUIS STEVENSON

Treasure Island

Edited by Jonathan Kelley,
with an Afterword by Bill Blauvelt

 THE TOWNSEND LIBRARY

TREASURE ISLAND

TP THE TOWNSEND LIBRARY

For more titles in the Townsend Library,
visit our website: **www.townsendpress.com**

Townsend Press, Inc.
1038 Industrial Drive
West Berlin, New Jersey 08091

ISBN 1-59194-038-9

Library of Congress Control Number:
2004111821

CONTENTS

PART 1: THE OLD PIRATE

PART 2: THE SEA COOK

PART 3: MY SHORE ADVENTURE

PART 4: THE STOCKADE

TREASURE ISLAND

PART 1

THE OLD PIRATE

CHAPTER 1

The Old Sea Dog at The Admiral Benbow

Squire Trelawney, Dr. Livesey, and some other gentlemen have asked me to tell the entire story of Treasure Island. I will keep nothing back except for the location of the island, for treasure still remains there. I, Jim Hawkins, am writing of these events in the year 17__. I will start by going back to the time when my father kept the Admiral Benbow Inn on the English coast and an old scarred seaman first came to lodge with us.

I remember him as if it were yesterday. He plodded to our door, a tall, strong, heavy, tanned man in a stained blue coat, pulling his sea chest behind him on a cart. His hair was pigtailed and tarred sailor-fashion, and his hands were scarred with black, broken nails. The white sword-scar on his cheek stood out clearly. He looked inside, whistling to himself. Then, in an odd high voice,

3

he broke out into a sea-song we would soon know well:

> **"Fifteen men on the dead man's chest—**
> **Yo-ho-ho, and a bottle of rum!"**

He rapped at our door. When my father appeared, the man called roughly for a glass of rum. It was brought. He drank slowly, savoring it while he looked around at the cliffs and at our signboard.

"This is a nice place for a grog-shop," said he after a time. "Do you get many visitors, mate?"

My father told him no, unfortunately, we got very few.

"Perfect," said he. "I'll stay here a bit. I'm a plain man who wants only rum, bacon, eggs and a high cliff to watch ships sail." My father hesitated, nervous to ask the normal questions. "And what might you call me, mate? 'Captain' will do. Oh, I see what you're waiting for—there!" and he threw down several gold pieces. "When I've spent those, tell me," he ordered fiercely.

In spite of his rough speech and his clothing, he didn't seem like a common sailor. Indeed, he seemed much more like a captain who was used to having his orders obeyed. We learned only a little: the morning before, the mail-coach had let him off at the Royal George. He had asked there about inns along the coast. Perhaps ours had been recommended, or described as lonely. For whatever reason, the seaman had chosen it from all the others.

He would say no more.

He spent his days hanging around the cove or on the cliffs with a brass telescope; in the evening he sat in a corner near the fire, drinking strong rum with a little water. If spoken to, he rarely answered except with a sudden, fierce look; then he would sort of growl through his nose like a foghorn. We, and our guests, learned to leave him alone.

Every day when he returned from his walk, he would ask if any other seafaring men had passed by. At first we thought he was looking for companionship, but soon we realized that he asked because he wished to avoid them. When another seaman stopped to lodge at the Admiral Benbow, the captain would carefully look him over through the curtains before coming into the parlor. Until the new sailor left, our man was quiet as a mouse.

One day he took me aside and promised me four silver pennies per month if I would keep a watch: should a one-legged sailor appear, I was to alert him right away. On the first of each month I asked him for my wages, and often he would simply give me a nose-growl and stare me down; but before the week was over, he always had second thoughts. He would pay me, then repeat his orders to look out for "the seafaring man with one leg."

The one-legged sailor haunted my dreams. On stormy nights, when the wind shook our house and the surf roared into the cove, I saw him in a thousand forms with a thousand evil expressions.

Sometimes his leg was cut off at the knee or hip; sometimes he was a sort of monstrous one-legged creature. The worst of the nightmares had him chasing me over hedges and ditches. In all, I paid a pretty high price for my monthly four pennies.

I was so terrified of my dreams of the one-legged sailor that the captain did not seem as frightening to me as he did to my parents and our customers. Some nights he drank too much rum, and would sit and sing his wicked, wild old sea-songs, ignoring everybody. But sometimes when drunk, he would call for rum for everyone present, and force them to gather around, either to sing with him or listen to his stories. Many a time did I hear the house shake with "Yo-ho-ho, and a bottle of rum," everyone joining in for dear life, trying to out-sing one another so as not to displease him. He was domineering and unpredictable. He would slap his hand on the table to demand silence; sometimes he would become angry at a question—at other times he would become angry because no questions were asked, assuming this to mean the group was not listening carefully to him. He would allow no one to go home until he had drunk himself sleepy and staggered off to bed.

His stories were what frightened people the most. He told dreadful tales of hangings, and walking the plank, and storms at sea, and the wild deeds and places in the pirate-infested Caribbean islands. If they were true, he had lived among the wickedest men in the history of the sea. His profanity shocked our guests' plain country ears, and my father felt that he would ruin us. Surely people would tire of coming here to be terrorized and sworn at. But I believe he was actually good for business. His frightening conduct was a fine bit of excitement in the quiet country life. Some of the younger men even pretended to admire him, calling him a "true sea dog" and a "real old salt," and saying he was the sort of man that made England a great sea-power.

In one way, at least, he did us serious financial harm. He stayed for months and months. The money he had paid when he arrived ran out, and my father never dared demand more. If he hinted at it, the captain gave a nose-growl so loud it was like a roar, staring my poor father out of the room. The annoyance and terror of those days surely hastened my father's early death.

The captain never changed his clothes all the time he lived with us. His cocked hat began to sag and lose shape, and he just let it hang. His coat developed holes, which he patched until it was mostly patches. He neither wrote nor received letters, and spoke only when drunk or demanding drink. None of us had ever seen him open the sea chest.

Only once did anyone cross him, near the end of my father's long illness. Dr. Livesey came in to see his patient, and accepted a bit of dinner afterward from my mother. He then went into the parlor to smoke a pipe until his horse was brought. I followed him in and was struck by the contrast: on the one hand was the neat, bright doctor, hair fashionably powdered white as snow, with dark eyes and pleasant manners; on the other was the filthy, heavy, bleary scarecrow of a drunken pirate captain, surrounded by simple country folk. The captain began to sing his usual song:

"Fifteen men on the dead man's chest—
Yo-ho-ho, and a bottle of rum!
Drink and the devil had killed all the rest—
Yo-ho-ho, and a bottle of rum!"

At first I had supposed "the dead man's chest" to be his big sea chest upstairs. It had been in many of my nightmares. But by now we were all used to the song—except for Dr. Livesey, who was talking with old Taylor, the gardener, about a new cure for his stiff joints. The doctor looked up angrily, then calmly continued his discussion. The captain, unused to being ignored, slapped the table in his customary demand for silence. He got it from everyone but Dr. Livesey, who kept speaking in a clear, kind voice in between draws on his pipe. The captain glared at him for a while, slapped the table again, glared even harder, and then swore and cried out in fury: "Silence there, between decks!"

"Were you addressing me, sir?" said the doctor.

"I was, blast you!" answered the ruffian.

The doctor replied in a professional tone, "I have only one thing to say to you, sir. If you keep on drinking rum, the world will soon be rid of a filthy scoundrel!"

The old fellow's fury was awful. He sprang to his feet, then drew and opened a sailor's pocketknife. "Silence, I say, or I'll pin you to the wall!" he bellowed.

The doctor stood his ground and spoke as calmly as before, so that the whole room might hear: "If you do not put that knife away this instant, I promise upon my honor that you shall hang next time court is in session."

They stared at each other for a bit, but the captain soon lost the battle of wills. He put up his weapon and sat down, grumbling like a beaten dog.

"And now, sir," continued the doctor, "take heed. I am a magistrate of this district as well as a doctor, and my job is to enforce the peace. I will have you watched day and night, and if I hear a single complaint about you for any reason—if you are even rude to anyone again—you will be hunted down and thrown out of town. Be warned."

Soon Dr. Livesey's horse was brought and he rode away, but the captain kept silent that evening, and for many evenings to come.

CHAPTER 2

BLACK DOG APPEARS
AND DISAPPEARS

Soon came the first of the mysterious events that eventually rid us of the captain, if not of his affairs. It was a bitter cold winter, with long, hard frosts and heavy gales. My poor father was bedridden and unlikely to survive until spring. Between caring for him and the inn, we were too busy to pay much attention to our unpleasant guest.

One frosty January morning, the captain arose early and went down the beach. As always, he had his cutlass and his brass telescope. As he walked away, he gave a loud indignant snort. Perhaps he was brooding over Dr. Livesey's warning.

Mother was upstairs with father while I set the breakfast table for the captain's return. As I was finishing, the parlor door opened. A pale stranger stepped in. He wore a cutlass, but did not have the look of a fighter, nor did he dress like a sailor. His left hand was missing two fingers. I always watched out for seafaring men, whether with one leg or two. This one puzzled me, for he had a sense of the sea about him despite his clothes.

I asked him what I could get for him. Rum, he said, but as I was going to fetch it, he sat down on a table and motioned me over. I paused where I was.

"Come here, sonny," he said. "Come nearer here."

I took a step nearer.

"Is this here table for my mate Bill?" he asked with a leer.

I told him I did not know his mate Bill, and this was for a guest in our house whom we called the captain.

"Well," said he, "my mate Bill would be called that. He has a cut on one cheek and a mighty pleasant manner, particularly when drinking. Does your captain have a cut on his right cheek? If so, he's my mate Bill. Now, is he here?"

I told him he was out walking.

"Which way has he gone, sonny?"

I pointed out the direction and told him when the captain was likely to return, and answered a few other questions.

"Ah, this'll be as good as drink to my mate Bill," said he with an unpleasant expression. I doubted that the captain would agree, but I did not know what to do and it was none of my business.

The stranger lingered just inside our door, peering around the corner. Once I went out into the road, but he immediately called me back. When I was slow to obey, he cursed and ordered me back right now.

As soon as I was back, his half fawning, half sneering manner returned. He patted my shoulder, called me a good boy. "I have a son of my own," he said. "Looks a lot like you, and the pride of my heart he is. But boys need discipline, sonny—discipline. If you had sailed with Bill, you wouldn't have had to be told twice, bless his heart. And look out there, sonny"—he nodded toward the beach—"yes, there's my mate Bill now, with his spyglass under his arm. You and me'll go behind the door, sonny, and we'll give Bill a little surprise, bless his heart."

So saying, the stranger backed into the parlor, taking me with him. He put me behind him in the corner so we were both hidden by the open door. The stranger seemed frightened and that made me very uneasy and alarmed. He made sure his cutlass was loose and ready, and kept trying to swallow away a lump in his throat.

At last the captain arrived. He slammed the door behind him without looking right or left and marched straight toward his waiting breakfast.

"Bill," said the stranger, trying to sound bold.

The captain spun around and confronted us. His face was suddenly pale and old-looking, like a man who has seen a ghost. Upon my word, I felt sorry for him.

"Come, Bill, surely you know an old ship-mate," said the stranger.

The captain gasped. "Black Dog!" he said.

"And who else?" returned the other, more at ease. "Black Dog, come to see his old shipmate Billy at the Admiral Benbow Inn. Ah, Bill, Bill, we have seen some times, us two, since I lost them two talons," holding up his mutilated hand.

"Now, look here," said the captain. "You've run me down. Speak up; what is it?"

"That's you, Bill," replied Black Dog, "you have it right. I'll have a glass of rum from this dear child here, who I've took such a liking to. We'll sit down and talk square, like old shipmates."

When I returned with the rum, they were already seated at the captain's breakfast table—Black Dog nearest the door, keeping one eye on his old shipmate and one on the exit. He told me to go away, but leave the door open. "Don't want you listening at the keyhole, sonny," he said. I obeyed and went into the bar.

I tried hard to listen anyway, but for a long time I heard only low voices. At last the voices grew louder, and I could pick up a few of the captain's curses.

"No, no, no, no; and an end of it!" he cried once. And again, "If it comes to hanging, hang all, say I."

Then there was a tremendous explosion of swearing and other noise—the chair and table went over in a thump, a clash of steel, and then a cry of pain. The next instant I saw Black Dog in full flight with a bloody cut on his left shoulder, and the captain hotly pursuing. Both had drawn cutlasses. Just at the door the captain aimed one last tremendous cut, which would certainly have split Black Dog wide open had it not struck our big signboard of Admiral Benbow. You can see the notch on the lower frame to this day.

The battle was over. In spite of his wound, Black Dog ran swiftly and disappeared over the edge of the hill in half a minute. The captain stood staring at the signboard like a bewildered man. Then he passed his hand over his eyes several times and at last turned back into the house.

"Jim," he said, "rum." As he spoke, he reeled a little, and caught himself with one hand against the wall.

"Are you hurt?" I cried.

"Rum," he repeated. "I must get away from here. Rum! Rum!"

I ran to fetch it, but my hands shook. I broke one glass and spilled a lot of rum. I heard a loud fall in the parlor. I ran in to find the captain lying full-length on the floor. At this point my mother, alarmed by the commotion, came running downstairs to help me. Between us we raised his head. He was breathing very loud and hard, but his eyes were closed and his face a horrible color.

"Deary me," cried my mother, "what a disgrace! And your poor father sick!"

We had no idea how to help the captain. We assumed he had gotten hurt in the scuffle. I got the rum and tried to put it down his throat, but his teeth were clamped tightly shut. To our great relief, Dr. Livesey soon came in for his regular visit to my father.

"Oh, doctor," we cried, "what shall we do? Where is he wounded?"

"Wounded? Fiddlesticks!" said the doctor. "The man has had a stroke, as I warned him. Now, Mrs. Hawkins, run upstairs and reassure your husband, while telling him nothing about it. As for me, I must do my best to save this fellow's worthless life. Jim, get me a bowl."

When I got back with the bowl, the doctor had already ripped up the captain's sleeve and exposed his great, tattooed arm. "Here's luck," "A fair wind," and "Billy Bones his fancy," were very neatly and clearly inked. Up near the shoulder there was a sketch of a man hanging from a gallows.

"Prophetic," the doctor said, touching this picture with his finger. "And now, Master Billy Bones, if that is your name, we'll have a look at the color of your blood. Jim, are you afraid of blood?"

"No, sir," I said.

"Then hold the basin." Saying this, he took

his sharp surgical knife and opened a vein.

A great deal of blood was taken before the captain opened his eyes and looked mistily about him. First he recognized the doctor with an unmistakable frown; then his glance fell upon me, and he looked relieved. But suddenly his color changed, and he tried to raise himself, crying, "Where's Black Dog?"

"There is no Black Dog here," said the doctor. "You have been drinking, against my advice, and have had a stroke. Very much against my will, I have dragged you out of the grave. Now, Mr. Bones—"

"That's not my name," he interrupted.

"I don't care," replied the doctor. "It's the name of a pirate I know, and I will call you that. Hear me, Mr. Bones: one glass of rum won't kill you, but if you take one you'll take another and another. I'll bet my wig that if you keep drinking, you'll soon be in Hell—do you understand that? Now make an effort, and I'll help you to your bed."

Between us, with much trouble, we managed to hoist him upstairs. When we laid him on his bed, his head fell limply back on the pillow.

"Now, mind you," said the doctor, "I clear my conscience. For you, rum is death." With that he took my arm and went to see my father.

As soon as he had closed the door he said to me, "I have drawn enough blood to keep him

quiet for a while; he should lie still for a week—
that is the best thing for him and for everybody
else. One more stroke will be his last."

CHAPTER 3

THE BLACK SPOT

About noon I stopped at the captain's door with some cool drinks and medicines. He was still weak, but awake and excited.

"Jim," he said, "you're the only one here worth anything, and I've always been good to you. Every month I've given you your pay. Now, mate, you see the shape I'm in, deserted by all. Surely you'll bring me a cup of rum, matey?"

"The doctor—" I began.

He cursed the doctor in a feeble voice. "Doctors is all louts," he said. "What does that doctor know about seafaring men? I been in places hot as pitch, and mates dying of yellow fever, and the land heaving with earthquakes. What can the doctor know of lands like that? Rum's been meat and drink, and man and wife, to me. Without my rum now I'm a poor old ship driven onto the rocks. I'll die, Jim, on your conscience, and that lout of a doctor's." He went on awhile, cursing and pleading. "Look, Jim, how my fingers shakes," he continued. "I haven't had a drop this blessed day. That doctor's a fool, I tell you. If I don't have rum, Jim, I'll have the horrors. I seen some of 'em already. I seen old Flint in the corner there, behind you, plain as day. If I get the horrors, it'll be mighty unpleasant for everybody. Your doctor hisself said one glass wouldn't hurt me. I'll give you a golden pound for a cup, Jim."

I was alarmed for my father, who needed quiet, and I was reassured by the doctor's words. The idea of a bribe, however, offended me. "I want none of your money," said I, "except what you owe my father. I'll get you one glass, and no more."

When I brought it to him, he seized it greedily and drank it down.

"Aye," said he, "that's better, sure enough. And now, matey, did that doctor say how long I was to lie here?"

"A week at least," I said.

"Thunder!" he cried. "A week! I can't do that; they'd have the black spot on me by then. Those lubbers will soon know where I am. They couldn't keep what they had, so they want what is mine. That's unseamanly behavior, I say. But I'm thrifty. I never wasted good money, and I'll trick 'em again. I'll put up full sails and escape 'em."

As he spoke, he had clamped onto my shoulder

so hard it hurt. Now he sat up from the bed with great difficulty. His spirited words contrasted with his weak voice.

"That doctor's done me wrong," he murmured. "My ears is ringing." He soon fell back onto the bed and lay silent awhile.

"Jim," he said at length, "you saw that seafaring man today?"

"Black Dog?" I asked.

"Ah! Black Dog," he muttered. "*He's* a bad 'un. But worse men sent him. If they send me the black spot, it means they're after my old sea chest. Jim, if that happens you get as fast as you can to that lout of a doctor. Tell him to call all hands, magistrates and such, to the Admiral Benbow. He'll run them all in, all of old Flint's crew that's left. I was old Flint's first mate, and I'm the only one who knows the location. Flint gave it to me when he lay a-dying at Savannah, like I am now. But don't go for the doctor unless they give me the black spot, or you see that Black Dog again, or a seafaring man with one leg, Jim—him above all."

"But what is the black spot, captain?" I asked.

"That's a summons, mate. I'll tell you if it comes. But you keep your eye out, Jim, and I'll share equals with you, upon my honor."

He wandered a little longer, his voice growing weaker. He took the medicine like a child, remarking that if ever a seaman needed medicine, it was he. Then he fell into a heavy sleep. Had fate not stepped in, I do not know what I would have done next—probably taken the whole tale to the doctor, in case the captain regretted his confession and tried to do away with me.

Unfortunately, my poor father died quite suddenly that evening. Our grief, the visits from the neighbors, the funeral arrangements, and keeping the inn running kept me and my mother busy. There was no time to worry over the captain.

He got downstairs next morning and had his meals as usual, though he ate little and had more rum than usual. He helped himself from the bar, scowling and blowing through his nose so that no one dared object. The night before the funeral he was as drunk as ever. It was shocking to hear his old sea-song while the house was mourning, but we were afraid, and the doctor was busy with a case far away. The captain seemed to weaken, holding onto the walls for support and breathing hard like a man on a steep mountain. He ignored me, and I think he had forgotten what he told me. But in spite of his weakness, his temper was more violent than ever. When he was drunk, he would often draw his cutlass and lay it bare on the table in front of him. He seemed shut up in his own world, ignoring others. And his mind seemed to wander. Once, to our amazement, he sang a country love-song he must have learned as a youth before he went to sea.

The day after the funeral, it was frosty and

foggy. At about three o'clock I was standing at the door for a moment, thinking about my father, when a hunched, aged-looking figure came slowly down the road. He was blind, tapping in front of him with a stick, eyes and nose shaded. He wore a huge old tattered sea-cloak. Never before had I seen a more deformed, dreadful-looking figure.

He stopped near the inn, and in an odd singsong voice spoke to the air: "Will any kind friend tell a poor blind man, who has lost his eyes defending his country—God bless King George!—where he is now?"

"You are at the Admiral Benbow, Black Hill Cove, my good man," I said.

"I hear a young voice," he said. "Will you give me your hand, my kind young friend, and lead me in?"

I held out my hand, and the creature gripped it like a vise. I was startled and tried to get loose, but the blind man pulled me close.

"Now, boy," he said, "take me in to the captain."

"Sir," I said, "I dare not."

"Take me in or I'll break your arm," he sneered. He wrenched it hard, and I cried out.

"Sir," said I, "it is for your sake. The captain is not himself. He sits with a drawn cutlass. Another gentleman—"

"Come, now, march," he interrupted. The cruel, cold, ugly voice scared me more than the pain, and I obeyed, walking in toward the parlor, where our sick old pirate was sitting in a rummy haze. The blind man clung close, leaning much of his weight on me. "Lead me straight up to him, and when I'm in view, cry out, 'Here's a friend of yours, Bill.' If you don't, I'll do this," and he twisted my arm so hard I thought I might faint. I was so terrified of the blind beggar that I forgot my terror of the captain. I opened the parlor door and, voice trembling, said what I had been ordered.

The poor captain raised his eyes. At once his

face went both cold sober and deathly sick. He moved to rise but could not.

"Now, Bill, sit where you are," said the beggar. "I can't see, but I can hear a finger stirring. Business is business. Hold out your left hand. Boy, take his left hand by the wrist and bring it near to my right."

We both obeyed him to the letter, and I saw him pass something into the captain's palm.

"And now that's done," said the blind man. He suddenly let go of me, and skipped nimbly out of the inn. I could hear his stick tap-tap-tapping into the distance.

It was some time before we gathered our senses, but at length I let go his wrist. The captain looked sharply into his palm.

"Ten o'clock!" he cried. "Six hours. We'll foil them yet!" He sprang to his feet, but then reeled and put his hand to his throat. He swayed for a moment, then fell face down on the floor.

I ran to him at once, calling to my mother, but haste was in vain. The captain had died of a massive stroke. My reaction still surprises me, for I had never liked him, though I had begun to pity him. As soon as I saw that he was dead, I burst into a flood of tears. It was the second death I had known, and the sorrow of the first was still fresh in my heart.

CHAPTER 4

THE SEA CHEST

Now I hastened to do as I should have before: tell my mother the whole tale. Our position was difficult and dangerous. The captain owed us money, but we doubted that the captain's old colleagues would care. I could not go to fetch Dr. Livesey without leaving my mother alone and unprotected. We felt unsafe in the house. Every noise filled us with fear. The house seemed haunted by approaching footsteps. The captain's corpse did nothing to calm our nerves, and I knew that horrible blind beggar was nearby. Our only option was to run to the nearby village for help. This we did, bareheaded in the frosty evening fog.

The village lay several hundred yards away, just on the other side of the next cove. Luckily, the blind man had come from the other direction. Our trip did not take long, though sometimes we stopped to clutch one another and listen. We heard nothing unusual—just the low wash of the waves.

How the sight of evening candles in windows cheered me! Unfortunately, that was all the help we got from a village of cowards. Not a single soul would agree to return with us to the Admiral Benbow. Some of them had heard of Captain Flint, and all were too terrified to come. Some farmhands working near the road recalled having seen some sinister strangers; the strangers had looked so fierce that the farmhands would not risk seeing them again. One villager had also seen what looked like a smuggler's ship in a nearby inlet. Several were willing to ride to Dr. Livesey's, which was in another direction, but not a single person would help us defend the inn.

When each had said his say, my mother had hers. She would not, she declared, lose money that belonged to her fatherless boy. "If none of the rest of you dare," she said, "Jim and I do. We will go back, and small thanks to you big, hulking, chicken-hearted men. We'll have that chest open if we die for it. And I'll thank you for that bag, Mrs. Crossley, to bring back our lawful money in."

Of course I said I would go with my mother, and of course they all said it was foolish. But not one man could be shamed into coming. All they would do was to give me a loaded pistol in case we were attacked and to promise to have horses saddled in case we returned with men in pursuit. One lad said he would ride to the doctor's to fetch armed assistance.

My heart was beating hard when we headed homeward. A full, rising moon peered through the upper edges of the icy fog. This made us hurry, for fog was our ally tonight and moonlight our enemy. We slipped along the hedges, noiseless and swift, detecting nothing sinister. Soon we were safely inside the Admiral Benbow.

I bolted the door at once, and we stood and panted for a moment in the dark, alone in the house with the dead captain's body. Then my mother got a candle, and holding hands we advanced into the parlor. He lay as we had left him, with his eyes open and one arm stretched out.

"Shut the curtain, Jim," whispered my mother. "They might come and watch outside." When I had done so she said, "Now we have to get the key off *that*; but who can stand to touch it?" and she gave a kind of sob.

I went down on my knees at once. On the floor by his hand there was a little round piece of paper, blackened on one side. No doubt this was the BLACK SPOT, and on the other side of it was written in a clear hand: "You have until ten tonight."

"He had until ten, Mother," said I; and just as I said it, our old clock struck. It startled us badly at first, but then reassured us, for it was only six.

"Now, Jim," she said, "that key."

I felt in his pockets. A few small coins, sewing tools, a plug of tobacco, his pocketknife, a compass, and a tinder box, but no key. I began to despair.

"Perhaps it's round his neck," suggested my mother.

Overcoming my disgust, I tore open his shirt at the neck. Sure enough, there was the key on a bit of tarred string. I cut it with the pocketknife and we hurried upstairs to his little room.

His timeworn sea chest looked like any other sailor's. The initial "B" was burned on the top of it with a hot iron.

"Give me the key," said my mother. She managed to turn it in the stiff lock and immediately threw back the lid.

A strong smell of tobacco and tar rose from the interior, but on top was only a suit of very good new clothes, carefully brushed and folded. Then came miscellaneous things: a tin box, sticks of tobacco, two pair of fine pistols, two brass compasses, an old Spanish watch, and other typical sailors' possessions. Most of it was of little value.

We kept digging, and eventually reached an old boat-cloak white with sea salt. My mother impatiently pulled it up to reveal the last things in the chest: a bundle of papers tied up in oilcloth and a canvas bag jingling with gold.

"I'll show these rogues that I'm an honest woman," said my mother. "I'll have my dues, and not a penny more. Hold Mrs. Crossley's bag." And she began to count out what the captain owed.

It was a long, difficult business, for the gold coins were of all countries and sizes—Spanish doubloons and pieces of eight, French *louis d'ors*, English guineas, and others, all mixed up. To make it harder, there were not many guineas, and they were the only coins whose exact value she knew.

When we were about halfway through, I suddenly put my hand on her arm, for I had heard a sound that brought my heart into my mouth—the tap-tapping of the blind man's stick upon the frozen road. We held our breaths as it drew nearer and nearer. Then it rapped on the inn door, and we could hear the handle being turned and the bolt rattling as the wretch tried to enter. All was silent for a long time, then the tapping began again. To our relief, it began to die away and we heard it no more.

"Mother," said I, "take it all and let's be going." I was sure the bolted door must have seemed suspicious and would likely bring the whole hornet's nest on us. Even so, I was thankful I had bolted it, as would anyone be who had ever met that terrible blind man.

But even in her fright, my mother obstinately refused. She knew her rights. And she would take no more nor less than the seven guineas we were owed, and she had not found them yet. We were arguing over it when we heard a little low whistle some distance away.

That was more than enough for both of us. "I'll take what I have," she said, jumping to her feet.

"And I'll take this to settle the bill," I said, picking up the oilcloth packet.

Soon we were both groping downstairs, leaving the candle by the empty chest. The minute we had the door open we got moving, and none too soon. The mist was lifting, the moon bright. Only around our door and in the nearby valley were there still a few wisps of fog to hide our escape. Worse, we heard the sound of several footsteps running. I looked back toward the sound and saw a light bounced back and forth, as a lantern does when its carrier is running.

"My dear," said my mother suddenly, "take the money and run on. I am going to faint."

This was certainly the end for both of us, I thought. How I cursed the neighbors' cowardice; how I blamed my poor mother for her honesty and her greed, for her past foolhardiness and present weakness! We were just at the little bridge, fortunately, and I helped her totter to the edge of the bank. She fainted away on my shoulder. Somehow I managed to drag her, I fear roughly, down the bank and partly under the bridge. There we had to stay even though we were in easy earshot of the inn, and not hard to see, if anyone nosed around.

CHAPTER 5

THE LAST OF THE
BLIND MAN

My curiosity soon overcame my fear, so I crept back up the bank. There I hid to watch the road, sheltered by a bush. Just after I was in position, our enemies came running, seven or eight all told. One was out front with the lantern; three ran together hand in hand. The blind beggar in the middle spoke.

"Down with the door!" he cried.

"Aye, aye, sir!" answered two or three. They rushed the door but found it unlocked. The blind man issued new commands in a voice filled with eagerness and rage.

"In, in, in!" he shouted, cursing them for their delay.

Four or five obeyed at once; two remained in the road with him. A moment later a voice shouted, "Bill's dead!"

The blind man cursed their delay some more. "Some of you lazy lubbers, search him. The rest of you go aloft and get the chest," he cried.

I could hear their footsteps on our old stairs, then fresh sounds of astonishment. The captain's window was thrown open so hard it broke, and a man leaned out into the moonlight to address the blind beggar.

"Pew," he cried, "they've been here before us. Someone's turned the chest out."

"Is it there?" roared blind Pew.

"The money's there."

The blind man cursed the money. "Flint's map, I mean," he cried.

"It ain't here," returned the man.

"You below there, is it on Bill?" cried the blind man again.

Another fellow came to the door of the inn. "Bill's been overhauled a'ready," he said. "Nothin' left."

"It's these people of the inn—it's that boy. I wish I had put his eyes out!" cried Pew, banging his stick on the road. "They were just here. Scatter, lads, and find 'em! Tear the house apart!"

There was a great racket through our old inn, heavy feet pounding, furniture thrown over, doors kicked in. Eventually the men came out, reporting that we were nowhere to be found. I then heard a whistle, the same one that had startled us while looking through the dead man's money, but repeated twice. To judge by the pirates' reaction, it was a danger signal from the hill near the village.

"There's Dirk again," said one. "Twice! We'll have to move, mates."

"Wait, you scum!" cried Pew. "Dirk is a fool and a coward. Ignore him. The inn people can't be far. You have them in your hands. Scatter and look for them, dogs! Oh, shiver my soul," he cried, "if I had eyes!"

This appeal produced some effect but not much. Two of the fellows began to look half-heartedly around the outside of the inn. But they seemed more concerned with their own danger. The rest loitered in the road.

"You have your hands on thousands, you fools, and you drag your feet! You'd be as rich as kings if you could find it. You know it's here, and you stand there skulking. None of you dared face Bill, and I did it—a blind man! You'll cost me my chance! I'm to be a poor, crawling beggar, mooching rum, when I might be riding in a coach! If you had the courage of a cockroach, you would catch them."

"Hang it, Pew, we've got the doubloons!" grumbled one.

"They might have hid the blessed thing," said another. "Take the loot, Pew, and don't stand here squalling."

Squalling was the word for it. Pew lost his temper, striking blindly left and right and managing to hit a couple of them. They cursed him back, threatened him horridly, and tried in vain to wrest the stick from his grasp.

This quarrel saved us, for while it was still raging, another sound came from the top of the lookout's hill—the gallop of horses. Almost at the same time a pistol-shot rang out from the hedge side. That was plainly the last signal of danger, for the pirates scattered in every direction, leaving Pew to tap up and down the road in a frenzy. He groped about, calling for his comrades. Finally he took a wrong turn and ran a few steps past me toward the village. "Johnny! Black Dog! Dirk!" he called out. "You won't leave old Pew, mates—not old Pew!"

Just then four or five riders came in sight and swept at full gallop down the slope. Pew heard, turned with a scream, and ran straight for the ditch. He fell down, but got quickly to his feet and made another dash. In his confusion, he ran directly into the path of the nearest rider.

The horseman tried to avoid him, but in vain. Down went Pew under the hooves with a terrible cry of despair. He fell on his side, then gently collapsed onto his face and moved no more.

I leaped to my feet and hailed the riders, who were pulling up to investigate the accident. One was the lad that had gone from the village to Dr. Livesey's. The rest I knew to be Royal revenue officers, whom the lad had met on his way and sensibly brought at once. Led by Supervisor

Dance, they had been riding to investigate the news of the smuggling-ship at Kitt's Hole. To this my mother and I owed our lives. I told Mr. Dance the story as we carried her to the village.

Pew was stone dead. My mother was far better; once in the village, a little cold water revived her. I knew she had recovered from her terrifying experience when she continued to complain of what she was owed. In the meantime the supervisor raced for Kitt's Hole. Once there, his men had to coax their horses down a steep slope, always watching for ambushes. The vessel, a type of coastal ship called a lugger, was already heading out even as Supervisor Dance hailed her.

A voice replied from the lugger, telling the officer to keep in cover unless he wanted some lead in him. A bullet whistled close by his arm. Soon after, the lugger disappeared. Mr. Dance sent a man to alert the revenue cutter that patrolled our coast, then returned to the village and told us of the lugger's escape. "It's just about useless. They've got clean away, and that's that. But I'm glad I stepped on Master Pew's feet."

I went back with him to the Admiral Benbow. It was completely smashed up; they had even thrown the clock over. The men had only the captain's moneybag and the silver from our till, but I could see that we were ruined. Mr. Dance could not determine their full motives.

"They got the money, you say? Well, then,

Hawkins, what in fortune were they after? More money, I suppose?"

"No, sir, I think not," replied I. "Sir, I believe I have it in my pocket; and I would like to have it put safely away."

"To be sure, boy; quite right," said he. "I'll take it, if you like."

"I thought perhaps Dr. Livesey—" I began.

"Perfectly right," he interrupted very cheerily, "perfectly right—a gentleman and a magistrate. I must ride and report to the doctor or the squire anyway. I don't regret Master Pew's death, of course, but people are always ready to find fault with an officer of his Majesty's revenue if they can. If you like, Hawkins, I'll take you along."

I thanked him heartily for the offer, and we walked back to the village where the horses were. By the time I had told mother of my intent the revenue officers were all in the saddle.

"Dogger," said Mr. Dance to one of his men, "you have a good horse; carry this lad behind you."

As soon as I was mounted, holding on to Dogger's belt, the supervisor gave the word, and the party struck out at a bouncing trot toward Dr. Livesey's house.

CHAPTER 6

THE CAPTAIN'S PAPERS

We rode hard all the way to Dr. Livesey's door. The front of the house was dark.

Mr. Dance told me to jump down and knock. I did, and asked the maid if Dr. Livesey was in. He was up at the squire's estate, dining with the squire, she said.

"That's where we'll go, boys," said Mr. Dance.

Rather than remount, I ran alongside Dogger to the nearby white line of hall buildings. Mr. Dance dismounted and took me into the house.

The servant led us to a great library. Here sat Squire Trelawney and Dr. Livesey, smoking pipes on either side of a bright fire.

I had never seen the squire so near. He was over six feet tall, broad-shouldered with a rough-and-ready face lined by his long travels. His black

38

eyebrows moved restlessly, giving him a look of some temper—not bad, but perhaps impulsive.

"Come in, Mr. Dance," he said, in a stately and condescending voice.

"Good evening, Dance," the doctor said with a nod. "And good evening to you, friend Jim. What good wind brings you here?"

The supervisor reported his story to these authorities. The two gentlemen leaned forward and listened with interest. When they heard how my mother went back to the inn, Dr. Livesey slapped his thigh in approval, and the squire cried "Bravo!" Long before the story was done, Mr. Trelawney was up pacing about. The doctor had removed his powdered wig as if to hear better. How strange he looked to me in his own short black hair.

At last Mr. Dance finished the story.

"Mr. Dance," said the squire, "you are a very noble fellow, and your conduct here deserves only praise. As for that worthless criminal, sir, riding him down was like stamping on a cockroach. This lad Hawkins is a fine one, I perceive. Hawkins, will you ring that bell? Mr. Dance must have some ale."

"And so, Jim," said the doctor, "you have what they were after, do you?"

"Here it is, sir," I said, and gave him the oil-cloth packet.

The doctor seemed eager to open it, but instead put it quietly in his coat pocket.

"Squire," he said, "when Dance has had his ale he must get back to his Majesty's service; but I mean to have Jim Hawkins sleep at my house. With your permission, I suggest we have the cold pie brought for him."

"Yes, Livesey," said the squire, "but Hawkins has earned better than cold pie."

So a big pigeon pie was brought before me, and I ate with the hunger of a hawk. Mr. Dance's conduct was further complimented, and he was at last dismissed.

"And now, Squire," said the doctor.

"And now, Livesey," said the squire in the same breath.

"One at a time, one at a time," laughed Dr. Livesey. "You have heard of this Flint, I suppose?"

"Heard of him!" cried the squire. "He was the bloodthirstiest pirate ever. Next to Flint, Blackbeard was a child. The Spaniards were so afraid of him, sir, that at times I was proud he was an Englishman. I saw his topsails off Trinidad, and our cowardly captain sailed us right back into Port of Spain."

"Well, I've heard of him," said the doctor. "But did he have money?"

"Money!" cried the squire. "Have you been deaf? For what would these villains risk their rascal carcasses but money?"

"We shall soon know," replied the doctor, "assuming you calm down long enough for me to ask. Let us suppose I have some clue as to the location of Flint's buried treasure. Would it amount to much?"

"Amount, sir!" cried the squire. "If we have such a clue, I will fit out a ship in Bristol dock, and take you and Hawkins here along, and I'll have that treasure if I have to search a year."

"Very well," said the doctor. "Now, then, if Jim agrees, we'll open the packet." He laid it on the table.

The bundle was sewn together. The doctor cut the stitches with his medical scissors, revealing two things—a book and a sealed paper.

"First of all we'll try the book," observed the doctor. He kindly motioned me to come join the squire in reading over his shoulder.

On the first page there were only some doodles and bits of misspelled writing, like those of a bored and uneducated man. One was the same as the tattoo mark, "Billy Bones his fancy"; then there was "Mr. W. Bones, mate," "No more rum," "Off Palm Key he got itt," and some other meaningless bits. I could not help wondering who had "got itt." "Itt" was probably a knife in the back.

"Not much there," said Dr. Livesey, and he turned the page.

The next ten or twelve pages were filled with a curious series of entries. There was a date at one end of the line and at the other a sum of money, as in account-books, but in place of the explanation between date and sum there was only a varying number of crosses. For example, on June 12, 1745, a sum of seventy pounds had plainly been owed someone, with only six crosses to explain why. In a few cases a place name was added, such as "Offe Caraccas." Others had bearings—locations described through entries of latitude and longitude, that is—like 62° 17' 20", 19° 2' 40".

The record lasted over nearly twenty years, with the amounts growing larger as time went on. At the end there were five or six wrong additions scratched out, and a total explained by these words: "Bones, his pile."

"I can't make sense of this," said Dr. Livesey.

"Clear as noonday," cried the squire. "This is the pirate's account-book. These crosses stand for the names of ships they sank or towns they plundered. The sums are the scoundrel's share, and he clarified in places. 'Offe Caraccas,' now; you see, here was some unhappy vessel boarded along the Spanish Main. God help the poor souls that manned her—long dead, certainly. Most of these bearings are located in the Caribbean."

"Right!" said the doctor. "Your travel experience is the key. And note how the amounts increased as he rose in rank."

There was little else in the volume but a few unexplained bearings and a table for converting between French, English, and Spanish money.

"Thrifty man!" cried the doctor. "He wasn't one to be cheated."

"And now," said the squire, "for the other."

The paper had been sealed in several places with wax. The doctor opened the seals with great care, and out fell the complete map of an island. It had bearings, the depth of the water, names of hills and bays and inlets: all the information needed to safely anchor a ship there. It was about nine miles long and five across, shaped like a fat dragon standing up, with two fine sheltered harbors. A hill in the center part was marked "The Spyglass." There were several later additions, but above all, three crosses of red ink: two on the north part of the island, one in the southwest. Beside this last, in the same red ink and in small letters much neater than the captain's, these words: "Bulk of treasure here."

On the back the same hand had written this further information:

Tall tree, Spyglass shoulder, bearing a point to the N. of N.N.E.

Skeleton Island E.S.E. and by E.

Ten feet.

The bar silver is in the north cache; you can find it by the trend of the east hummock, ten fathoms south of the black crag with the face on it.

The arms are easy found, in the sand-hill, N. point of north inlet cape, bearing E. and a quarter N.

J.F.

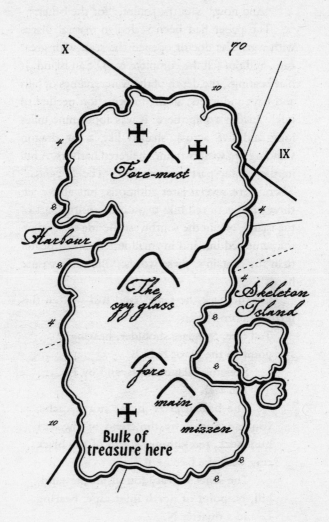

That was all. I understood none of it, but it filled the squire and Dr. Livesey with delight.

"Livesey," said the squire, "you will give up this wretched practice at once. Tomorrow I start for Bristol. In three weeks' time or less, sir, we'll have the best ship and crew in England. Hawkins shall come; he'll make a fine cabin boy. You, Livesey, are ship's doctor; I am admiral. We'll take Redruth, Joyce, and Hunter. We'll have favorable winds, a quick passage, and an easy time finding the spot. We'll be rolling in money."

"Trelawney," said the doctor, "I'll go with you, as will Jim; he'll be a fine man. There's only one man I'm afraid of."

"And who's that?" cried the squire. "Name the dog, sir!"

"You," replied the doctor, "for you cannot hold your tongue. We are not the only men who know of this paper. These fellows who attacked the inn tonight are bold and desperate, as are those who stayed aboard that lugger. They too are determined to get the money. We must take care, and never be alone. Jim and I shall stick together, and you should take Joyce and Hunter when you ride to Bristol. None of us must breathe a word of what we've found."

"Livesey," returned the squire, "you are right, as always. I'll be as silent as the grave."

TREASURE ISLAND

PART 2

THE
SEA COOK

CHAPTER 7

I Go to Bristol

All of our plans for swift sailing ran into snags. Dr. Livesey had to go to London to find a physician to run his practice, and I could not accompany him. The squire was hard at work in Bristol. I remained in the care of old Redruth, the gamekeeper, at the hall.

Though I was almost a prisoner, I was full of sea-dreams and imagination. I spent hours memorizing every detail of the map, exploring in my mind every acre of the island. The view from the hill called Spyglass changed every time: most often we were hunted by hostile natives or exotic animals. In fact, looking back I now realize that our actual adventures turned out far stranger and more tragic than any fantasy my mind could conjure.

Weeks passed. One day a letter came for Dr. Livesey. On the envelope was written: "To be opened by Tom Redruth or young Hawkins if Dr. Livesey is not available." Obeying this order, I read aloud the following important news:

Old Anchor Inn, Bristol
March 1, 17__

Dear Livesey—I do not know whether you are at the hall or still in London, so I have sent this to both places.

The ship is ready for sea. You never imagined a finer schooner than the two-hundred-ton *Hispaniola*, so handy that a child might sail her. I got her through my old friend, Blandly, who has been most helpful. He worked unceasingly in my interest, as did everyone in Bristol, as soon as they got wind of the port we sailed for—treasure, I mean.

"Redruth," I interrupted, "Dr. Livesey will not like that. The squire has been talking, after all."

"Well, who's got more right?" growled the gamekeeper. "Pretty odd if Dr. Livesey can boss the squire, I should think."

At that I gave up all attempts at commentary and read straight on:

Blandly himself found the *Hispaniola*, and got an absurdly low price for her. Some men in Bristol call Blandly dishonest and greedy. They say that the *Hispaniola* actually belonged to him, that he sold it to me ridiculously high. This is all transparent slander. None, however, dare deny the ship's seaworthiness.

The workmen, riggers and so on, were annoyingly slow. But what troubled me was the crew. I wanted a full complement of twenty men—in case of natives, pirates, or the French—and could hardly find half a dozen, until good fortune brought me the very man I needed.

I was standing on the dock when he happened by, sniffing appreciatively at the salt air. I learned that he was an old sailor who kept an inn and knew every seafaring man in Bristol. Life ashore was harming his health, and he sought to go to sea as a cook. I was most touched, and out of pity, I hired him then and there. His name is Long John Silver, and he has lost a leg in his country's service, sailing under the immortal Hawke.

What I did not realize was that I had found not merely a cook but a crew. Between Silver and myself, in a few days we gathered some of the toughest, ugliest old salts you can imagine. With these ferocious men I believe we could fight off a fully armed warship. Long John even got rid of two men I had already hired, showing me that they were unreliable fresh-water swabs.

I am in excellent health and spirits, yet I shall not enjoy a moment till I hear the clank of the capstan as we hoist anchor. Seaward, ho! Hang the treasure; I yearn for the glory of the sea.

Now, Livesey, waste no further time. Let young Hawkins go at once to see his mother, under Redruth's guard, then hurry to Bristol.

John Trelawney

Postscript—I did not tell you that Blandly, who is to send a vessel after us if we don't return by

September first, has found us a stiff but competent sailing-master. Long John Silver has
unearthed a very competent mate, named
Arrow. The *Hispaniola* shall have discipline
equal to the Navy.

I forgot to tell you that I investigated
Silver. He has a bank account, which he has
never overdrawn. He leaves his wife to manage the inn. She has a sharp tongue, and perhaps it is she that drives him back to sea.

J. T.

P.P.S.—Hawkins may stay one night with his
mother.

J. T.

You can fancy my excitement. Redruth was a
wet blanket. He did nothing but grumble, and I
despised him. Any of his subordinates would have
gladly taken his place, but the squire's orders were
law here. None but old Redruth would even have
dared complain.

The next morning we set out on foot for the
Admiral Benbow. I found my mother in good
health and spirits. The captain was beyond power
to do us harm. The squire had generously had
everything repaired and repainted and had bought
new furniture. He even found her an apprentice
boy to help her in my absence.

Seeing that boy made me realize for the first
time that I was leaving my mother, my home, and
all that I knew. At the sight of this clumsy stranger
I shed my first tears. I was too hard on him, for I

knew the work and he did not, and I found fault with his every activity.

The night passed, and after lunch the next day Redruth and I prepared to leave. I said good-bye to Mother, the cove where I had lived all my life, and the dear old Admiral Benbow Inn. I had one last thought of the captain striding down the beach all those times. Then we turned the corner and my home was out of sight.

The mail-coach picked us up about dusk at the Royal George. I was wedged in between Redruth and a stout old gentleman, and despite the swift motion and cold night air, I must have dozed from the beginning. At last I awoke to a poke in the ribs from Redruth. The coach was standing still in front of a large building in a city, and it looked to be mid-morning.

"Where are we?" I asked.

"Bristol," said Tom. "Get down."

Mr. Trelawney had lodged at a dockside inn to supervise the work on the schooner. We walked past ships of all types and sizes from many different countries. In one, sailors sang at their work; in another, men were high over my head hanging like spiders on thin-looking ropes. Somehow I had lived my entire life by the shore, yet never really been near the sea. The combined smell of tar and salt was new. I saw many old sailors, with rings in their ears, and tarred pigtails, and their swaggering, clumsy sea-walk. I would rather have seen them than kings or archbishops.

And I was going to sea myself, in a schooner with a piping boatswain and pigtailed singing seamen, bound for an unknown island to seek for buried treasure!

While I was still daydreaming, we arrived in front of a large inn and met Squire Trelawney, decked out in blue like a sea-officer. He was smiling, even walking like a sailor.

"Here you are," he cried, "and the doctor came last night from London. Bravo! The ship's company complete!"

"Oh, sir," I cried, "when do we sail?"

"Sail!" he replied. "We sail tomorrow!"

CHAPTER 8

At the Sign
of the Spyglass

When I finished breakfast the squire gave me a note to deliver to Mr. John Silver at a small dockside tavern named the Spyglass. I set off through the great crowds, overjoyed to see more of the ships and seamen.

Soon I found the tavern. Its sign was newly painted and there were red curtains on the windows. I peered in at the door. The place was full of noisy sailors and tobacco smoke. Soon I saw a man enter the main room, missing a leg at the hip, walking with a crutch. This must be Long John, I thought. He moved cheerfully among the tables, with many a merry word or a slap on the shoulder for his guests.

Now, in truth, the squire's description of Long John had stirred my fears. I had long watched out for a one-legged sailor at the old

Benbow. But after seeing the captain and Black Dog and blind Pew, I thought I knew the look of a pirate. This clean, pleasant landlord did not resemble those desperate men.

I gathered my courage, entered, and walked right up to the innkeeper. "Mr. Silver, sir?" I asked, holding out the note.

"Yes, my lad," he said, "that is my name. And who may you be?" And then he saw the squire's letter, and seemed startled. "Oh!" he said loudly, offering his hand. "Our new cabin boy! Pleased to see you." He took my hand in his large firm grasp.

Just then one of the customers at the far side rose suddenly and dashed out into the street. Even so, I had recognized him. He was the tallow-faced man, missing two fingers, who had come first to the Admiral Benbow.

"Oh," I cried, "stop him! It's Black Dog!"

"I don't care if he's Admiral Hawke himself!" cried Silver. "He hasn't paid. Harry, run and catch him." A man near the door leaped up to give chase, and Silver continued. "Who did you say he was?" he asked. "Black what?"

"Dog, sir," I said. Has Mr. Trelawney not told you of the pirates? He was one of them."

"Oh?" cried Silver. "In my house! Ben, run and help Harry. So he was one of those swabs? Was that you drinking with him, Morgan? Come here."

The old, gray-haired, tanned sailor came forward sheepishly, shifting his chewing tobacco.

"Now, Morgan," said Long John very sternly, "you never saw that Black—Black Dog before, did you, now?"

"Not I, sir," said Morgan with a salute.

"You didn't know his name, did you?"

"No, sir."

"That's good for you, Tom Morgan!" exclaimed the landlord. "If you had been mixed up with his kind, you would never set foot in my house again. And what was he saying to you?"

"I don't rightly know, sir," answered Morgan.

"Is that a head on your shoulders, or a rock?" cried Long John. "'Don't rightly know,' don't you! Come, now, what was he jawing—voyages, cap'ns, ships? What was it?"

"We was a-talkin' of keelhauling," answered Morgan.

"Keelhauling, was you? And a mighty suitable thing, too. Get back to your place, Tom, you lubber."

As Morgan rolled back to his seat, Silver whispered to me in a confidential tone: "He's quite an honest man, Tom Morgan, just stupid. And now," he ran on again, aloud, "let's see—Black Dog? No, I don't know the name. Yet I kind of think—yes, I've seen the swab. He used to come here with a blind beggar."

"I don't doubt that," said I. "I knew that blind man too. His name was Pew."

"It was!" cried Silver, now quite excited,

stumping up and down on his crutch. "Pew! That were his name for certain. He looked like a shark, he did! If we catch this Black Dog, now, there'll be news for Cap'n Trelawney! He talked o' keelhauling, did he? I'll keelhaul *him!*"

The sight of Black Dog had made me suspicious. I watched the cook closely, but his rantings were quite convincing. The two men soon came panting back, confessing failure; Silver scolded them as though they were thieves. I was convinced of his innocence.

"See here, now, Hawkins," said he, "what's Cap'n Trelawney to think, me having this wicked man sitting in my own house drinking my rum! And you tell me who he is, and I let him get away? Now, Hawkins, you do me justice with the cap'n. You're a smart lad, as I seen when you first come in. What could I do, with this missing leg? When I was a master mariner, I'd have come alongside him and brought him down for sure; but now—"

And then he stopped, and his jaw dropped as though he had remembered something.

"The money!" he burst out. "Three cups o' rum! Why, shiver my timbers, if I hadn't forgotten my money!" He sat down and began to laugh. I could not help joining, and we laughed together until the tavern rang.

"Why, what a precious old sea-calf I am!" he said at last, wiping his cheeks. "What was I thinkin'? Duty is duty, messmates. I'll put on my old sea-hat and go with you, Hawkins. I will report this here affair to Cap'n Trelawney myself. For this is serious, young Hawkins. And neither of us has come out of the affair with anything to our credit. But dash my buttons! That was a good 'un about my bill."

He began to laugh again, so heartily that I felt obliged to join him even though I did not see what was so funny.

On the way to see the squire, he told me all about the different ships that we passed by, their rigs, tonnages, and nationalities. He explained the work that was going on: loading and unloading, or making ready for sea. Now and then he would tell me some little sea-story, or teach me a nautical phrase until I learned it perfectly. I began to think him a great shipmate.

When we got to the inn, the squire and Dr. Livesey were seated together, finishing a quart of ale before inspecting the schooner.

Long John told the story from first to last, with a great deal of spirit and perfect truth. "That was how it were, now, weren't it, Hawkins?" he would say, now and again, and I could always verify his story.

The two gentlemen regretted that Black Dog had got away, but we all agreed there was nothing to be done. They complimented Long John for his effort to catch Black Dog and for his honesty in telling them the whole story. Then Long John took up his crutch and departed.

"All hands aboard by four this afternoon," shouted the squire after him.

"Aye, aye, sir," cried the cook.

"Well, squire," said Dr. Livesey, "I don't put much faith in your discoveries, as a general rule; but this John Silver suits me."

"The man's a good one," declared the squire.

"And now," added the doctor, "Jim may come onboard with us, may he not?"

"Certainly," the squire said. "Take your hat, Hawkins, and we'll see the ship."

CHAPTER 9

POWDER AND ARMS

We took a small boat out to the anchored *Hispaniola*. Mr. Arrow, the mate, saluted us as we boarded. Mr. Arrow was a tanned old sailor with an earring and a tendency to squint. He and the squire exchanged very friendly greetings.

A sailor followed us down into the cabin. "Captain Smollett, sir, asking to speak with you," said he.

"As he pleases. Show him in," said the squire.

The captain was close behind his messenger, looking angry. He entered and shut the door behind him.

"Well, Captain Smollett, what have you to say? All shipshape and seaworthy, I hope?"

"Well, sir," said the captain, "plain speech is best, even at the risk of offense. I don't like this cruise. I don't like the men and I don't like my officer."

"Perhaps, sir, you don't like the ship?" inquired the squire, angry in turn.

"I can't say until I have sailed her," said the captain. "She seems well-built."

"Possibly, sir, you may not like your employer, either?" the squire said.

Here Dr. Livesey cut in. "Calm down," he said. "Such questions only produce ill feelings. Captain, your words deserve an explanation. You say you don't like this cruise. Why?"

"I was hired, sir, on sealed orders, to sail this ship where that gentleman might order," said the captain. "Then I find that every deckhand knows more about our voyage than I do. Is that fair, sir?"

"No," Dr. Livesey said, "It isn't."

"Next," the captain said, "I learn—from my own crew, mind you—that we are going after treasure. Treasure voyages are ticklish and dangerous, and I don't like them. When everyone knows the secret but me, I like them even less."

"Continue," said the squire, still frostily.

"Very well," the captain answered. "I don't believe that either of you gentlemen realize how dangerous this mission is. Having the secret blabbed makes it even worse."

"That is all clear, and I daresay true enough," replied Dr. Livesey. "We accept the risk, but we are less ignorant than you think. Next, you say you don't like the crew. Are they not good seamen?"

"I don't like them, sir," returned Captain

Smollett. "And furthermore, I think I should have been allowed to choose them."

"Perhaps you should have been consulted," replied the doctor. "No offense was meant. And you don't like Mr. Arrow?"

"He's a good seaman, but too friendly with the crew to be a good officer. A mate must never be too familiar with the hands. He must be a symbol of authority, and this man is not."

"Very well, captain. What do you want?" asked the doctor.

"Well, gentlemen, are you determined to go on this cruise?"

"Like iron," answered the squire.

"Very good," said the captain. "Since you have heard me out patiently, sirs, let me go on. They are putting the powder and the arms in the fore hold. You have a good place under the cabin; why not put them there?—first point. You are bringing four of your own people with you, and they tell me some of them are to berth forward. Why not give them the berths here beside the cabin?—second point."

"Any more?" asked Mr. Trelawney.

"One more," said the captain. "There's been too much blabbing already."

"Far too much," agreed the doctor.

"I'll tell you what I've heard myself," continued Captain Smollett: "that you have a map of an island, with crosses to show where treasure is, and precisely where that the island lies."

"I never told that," cried the squire, "to a soul!"

"The hands know it, sir," returned the captain.

"Livesey, that must have been you or Hawkins," cried the squire.

"It doesn't much matter who it was," replied the doctor. None of us paid much regard to Mr. Trelawney's protest, for he was so careless in speech. But I believed at least that he had not told the specific location of the island to anyone. I knew I had not told, and surely the doctor had not. That could only mean the hands had already known.

"Well, gentlemen," continued the captain, "I don't know who has this map; but I believe it should be kept secret even from me and Mr. Arrow. If not, I ask you to accept my resignation."

"I see," said the doctor. "You wish us to keep this matter quiet, and to concentrate weapons in the ship's stern, near my friend's own people. In other words, you fear a mutiny."

"Sir," said Captain Smollett, "no offense, but you have no right to put words in my mouth. No competent captain would go to sea if he suspected a mutiny was in the wind. As for Mr. Arrow, I believe him thoroughly honest. And some of the men are honest—maybe even all of them. But I am responsible for the ship's safety and the life of every man aboard. When I see things going wrong, I must ask you to take precautions or let me resign my position. And that's all."

"Captain Smollett," began the doctor with a smile, "I hope you'll excuse me for saying this: I'll wager my wig that you came in here expecting you would lose your job for speaking so openly."

"Doctor," said the captain, "you are smart. I expected to be fired for speaking my mind. I had no idea Mr. Trelawney would listen."

"I wouldn't have," cried the squire. "If it hadn't been for Livesey, I would have sent you packing. As it is, I have heard you. I will do as you desire, but I think less of you."

"As you please, sir," said the captain. "You'll find I do my duty." With that he took his leave.

"Trelawney," said the doctor, "contrary to all my notions, I believed you have managed to get two honest men on board with you—that man and John Silver."

"Silver, perhaps," cried the squire. "As for that intolerable fake, I find his conduct unmanly, unsailorly, and downright un-English."

"Well," the doctor said, "we shall see."

When we came on deck, the men were shifting the arms and powder, supervised by the captain and Mr. Arrow.

I liked the new sleeping arrangements. The aft, or rear part of the main hold, had been converted to six cabins. These were only connected to the galley and forecastle—the forward crew quarters—by a corridor on the port side. Originally, the captain,

Mr. Arrow, Hunter, Joyce, the doctor, and the squire were going to occupy these. Now Redruth and I were to get two of them. Mr. Arrow and the captain would sleep in the small cabin on the quarterdeck. It was cramped, but had room for two hammocks, and even the mate seemed pleased. Perhaps he too had doubted the crew, but I cannot know for sure. As you shall hear, we did not long have the benefit of his opinion.

While the men were hard at work changing the powder and berths, Long John came alongside in a shore-boat with the last couple of crewmen. Our cook scrambled up the side in spite of his wooden leg. When he saw what was happening, he exclaimed, "So ho, mates! What's this?"

"We're a-changing the powder, Jack," answered one.

"Why, by the powers," cried Long John, "we'll miss the morning tide!"

"My orders!" said the captain shortly. "You may go below, my man, and prepare supper."

"Aye, aye, sir," answered the cook. He touched his forehead in salute and headed for his galley.

"He's a good man, captain," said the doctor.

"Very likely, sir," replied Captain Smollett. "Easy with that, men," he said to the fellows who were moving the powder. He then saw me examining the long nine-pounder swivel gun amidships, and said, "You, ship's boy! Get to work! Go and help the cook."

As I was hurrying off I heard him say quite loudly, to the doctor, "I'll have no favorites on my ship."

I shared the squire's opinion of the captain.

CHAPTER 10

THE VOYAGE

All that night we bustled about getting things ready. I had never worked half as hard in a night at the Admiral Benbow. The squire's friends, Mr. Blandly and the like, came out to wish him well. A little before dawn, the boatswain gave the signal and the crew raised the anchor. The ship was alive with brief commands, the shrill whistle of the boatswain's pipe, and the men hurrying in the glimmer of the lanterns. Even if I had been twice as tired, I would not have missed the moment for the world.

"Now, Barbecue, give us a song," cried one voice, to Silver.

"The old one," cried another.

"Aye, aye, mates," said Long John, standing by with his crutch under his arm. He sang out the words I knew so well:

"Fifteen men on the dead man's chest—"

The whole crew joined in:

"Yo-ho-ho, and a bottle of rum!"

That song carried me back to the old Admiral Benbow, and I could almost hear the voice of the captain joining in the chorus. Soon the anchor hung dripping at the bow. The sails began to draw wind. The land and ships began to move on either side, and before I could lie down to get some sleep the *Hispaniola*'s voyage to Treasure Island had begun.

The voyage was mostly easy and uneventful, so I will skip most of the details. The ship proved swift and solid, with a capable captain and crew. But before we came in sight of Treasure Island, some important things had happened.

Mr. Arrow turned out even worse than the captain had feared. After a day or two at sea he began to appear on deck obviously drunk. Often he was ordered below in disgrace. The men neither respected nor obeyed him, and did as they pleased. Sometimes he fell and cut himself; sometimes he lay all day long in his little bunk. Now and then he would sober up for a day or two and actually do his work.

Where he got the drink was the ship's mystery. When we asked him if he were drunk, he would laugh. Or, if he happened to be sober, he would solemnly state that he drank only water. As an officer he was worse than useless; he was a bad influence on the men. But he was not long for this world. Nobody was much surprised, nor very sorry, when one dark night in heavy seas he vanished.

"Overboard!" said the captain. "Well, gentlemen, that saves the trouble of putting him in irons."

But with our mate gone, someone had to be promoted. The boatswain, Job Anderson, was the best choice. He kept his old title but did the mate's job. Mr. Trelawney knew the sea, and in easy weather he often stood watch. The coxswain, Israel Hands, was an experienced old seaman who could perform any shipboard task. We made out well.

Israel Hands was close with Long John Silver, or Barbecue as the men called him. It was a wonder to watch our ship's cook manage. He carried his crutch by a cord round his neck, freeing both hands. He would wedge his crutch against the wall, swaying with the ship's motions, cooking just as if he were ashore. He got around on deck in even the heaviest weather with the aid of a couple of lines he rigged across the wide spaces. The crew called them Long John's Earrings, and he would hand himself across as quickly as others could walk.

Some of the men had sailed with him before, and all respected and obeyed him. "Barbecue's no common man," said the coxswain to me. "He had good schooling in his young days. And brave—a lion's nothing alongside of Long John! I seen him fight four men at once and knock their heads together—him unarmed." Long John knew just how to talk to each man, and did favors for everyone. He kept the galley spotlessly clean, even with his parrot in a cage in one corner.

He was especially kind to me. "Come away, Hawkins," he would say, "and have a talk with John. Nobody's more welcome than you, my son. Sit down and hear the news. Cap'n Flint—I calls my parrot Cap'n Flint, after the famous pirate— was just predicting success to our voyage. Wasn't you, cap'n?"

And the parrot would repeat: "Pieces of eight! Pieces of eight! Pieces of eight!" until John threw his handkerchief over the cage.

"Now, that bird," he would say, "is maybe two hundred years old, Hawkins—they live forever mostly; and only the devil's seen more wickedness. She's sailed with Edward England, the great pirate cap'n. She's been all over the world—Madagascar, Malabar, Surinam—any place you could name. It was at the salvage of the wrecked silver ships that she learned 'Pieces of eight,' and no wonder, Hawkins, they raised three hundred and fifty thousand pieces of eight! She's smelled plenty of gunpowder too. Didn't you, cap'n?"

"Stand by to go about," the parrot would scream.

"Ah, she's handsome, she is," he would say, and give her sugar from his pocket. The bird would peck at the cage and begin to swear. John would add, "You can't touch tar and stay clean, lad. Here's this poor old innocent bird o' mine swearing blue fire, and knowing nothing of it. She would swear the same before a chaplain." John would solemnly touch his forehead. I thought him the best of men.

In the meantime, the squire and Captain Smollett were still on unfriendly terms. The squire did not conceal his poor opinion of the captain, who himself never spoke except when spoken to, and then only sharp and short and dry. When the squire pressed, Smollett admitted that he seemed to have been wrong about the crew, that most had behaved fairly well. He loved the ship, praising her handling in the wind, but he would always add that he did not like the cruise. This always sent the squire away in a huff. "A trifle more of that man," he would say, "and I shall explode."

We hit some bad weather, but the *Hispaniola* proved to be a fine ship. The hands seemed content, as they should have been, for they were treated very well. Every other day they got pudding, and were given double rum at the least excuse, such as a man's birthday. A barrel of apples stood amidships for any man to help himself.

"No good has ever come of it," the captain said to Dr. Livesey. "Spoil the crew and you make devils of them."

But good did come of the apple barrel, as you shall hear. Without it, we might all have perished by treachery.

We had let the trade winds carry us far north of the island—I am not allowed to be more specific—and now we were running down toward it with a sharp lookout day and night. That night, or at the latest by tomorrow noon, we expected to sight Treasure Island. We were heading southsouthwest with a steady breeze and a quiet sea. Everyone was in fine spirits as we neared the end of the first part of our adventure.

Just after sundown, on my way to my berth, I decided to have an apple. I ran on deck. The men on watch were all forward, looking out for the island. The man at the helm watched the sails flap and whistled gently to himself. The only other sound was the swish of the sea.

My arm found no apples, so I climbed into the barrel. There were only a few left. I sat down and was soon rocked to sleep by the ship's motion, but was startled awake by a sort of clashing sound. I heard a man sit down, and felt the barrel shake as he leaned his shoulders against it. I listened; it sounded like two men. I was about to jump up when one began to speak.

It was Silver's voice, and before I had heard a dozen words, I knew I must not show myself. I lay there trembling, listening in fear and curiosity. From those first dozen words I understood that the lives of every honest man aboard depended upon me alone.

CHAPTER 11

What I Heard
in the Apple Barrel

"No, not I," said Silver. "Flint was cap'n; I was quartermaster. The same battle with a warship that took my leg took Pew's eyes. But we were luckier than Roberts' men—they hanged like dogs. But not us—Flint got us away safe."

"Ah!" cried an admiring voice. It was Dick, the youngest hand on board. "He was the best, was Flint!"

"Davis was a good man too, by all accounts," said Silver. "I never sailed with him; first with Cap'n England, then with Flint, and now here on my own account. I made nine hundred pounds sailing with England, and two thousand with Flint. I got it all saved in the bank—not bad for a seaman. Where's all England's men now? I dunno. Where's Flint's? Why, mostly here, and some of 'em were begging before that. Old Pew spent twelve hundred pounds in a year and used up all he had. Now he's dead, but for two years before that, the man was starving! He begged, and he stole, and he cut throats, and starved anyway!"

"So, money ain't much use, after all," said the young seaman.

"Nothing helps a fool," cried Silver. "But listen. You're young, but you're smart. I seen that right away, and I'll talk to you like a man."

You may imagine how I felt, hearing him flatter another with exactly the same words he had used on me. I would have liked to shoot him. He had no idea I was listening, of course, and kept on talking.

"Gentlemen of fortune lives rough, and they risk hanging, but they eat and drink lively. When a cruise is done, they has hundreds of pounds in their pockets. Most goes for rum and wild times, and when it runs out they're back at sea. Me, I saves it, some here, some there, none too much anywheres, so as not to raise suspicion. I'm fifty, mind you. After this cruise, I set up as a real gentleman. In the meantime I've lived comfortable-like. And how did I begin? As a common seaman, like you!"

"But all the other money's lost now, ain't it?" asked Dick. "It's in banks in Bristol, isn't it, and now you can't go back there."

"It were in banks," said the cook, "when we set sail. But my old missus has it all by now. And the Spyglass is sold, and the old girl's off to meet me. I would tell you where, for I trust you, but it'd make jealousy among the mates."

"And can you trust your missus?" asked Dick.

"Gentlemen of fortune," replied the cook, "usually don't trust each other, and rightly. But I have a way with me. Mates don't turn on old John. Flint's crew was the roughest bunch alive. But when I was quartermaster on his ship, they were gentle as lambs. I don't mean to boast, but you see how easy I am to get along with. Ah, you may be sure of yourself in old John's ship."

"Well, I tell you now," replied the lad, "I didn't like the job till I had this talk, John; but I'll shake on it now."

"And a brave lad you are, and smart too," answered Silver, shaking hands heartily enough to shake the barrel, "and a fine gentleman of fortune."

I had begun to understand their terms. A "gentleman of fortune" was a common pirate. Dick had been one of the honest hands—maybe the last one left aboard—and I had overheard his corruption. Soon Silver gave a little whistle, and I heard a third man stroll up and sit down.

"Dick's square," said Silver.

"Oh, I know'd Dick was square," answered the coxswain, Israel Hands. "He's no fool." I heard him spit. "But look here, Barbecue," he went on, "how long are we a-going to wait around? I've had enough o' Cap'n Smollett, by thunder!"

"Israel," said Silver, "your head ain't much use, but your ears is big enough, so listen. You'll keep sleeping forward, and living hard, and speaking soft, and wait till I give the word."

"I'm not saying no," growled the coxswain. "But when?"

"When?" cried Silver. "The last moment I can manage, that's when. We've Cap'n Smollett, a first-rate seaman, to sail the ship for us. The squire and doctor has a map—I don't know where it is, do you? Let this squire and doctor find the stuff, get it aboard, do all the work. If it was up to me, Cap'n Smollett'd navigate us halfway back again before I struck."

"Why? We're all seamen here. We can sail," said the lad Dick.

"We're all deckhands, you mean," snapped Silver. "We can steer a course, but who's to set one? That's what sets you apart. If I had my way, I'd have Cap'n Smollett work us back into the trade winds at least. That way we'd not get lost and run out of water. You ever been on a ration of a spoonful a day, seen men die of the thirst? But I know your minds. I'll finish 'em at the island, soon as the loot's onboard, though we're worse off because of it. You won't be happy till you're drunk. Makes my heart sick to sail with the likes of you!"

"Easy, Long John," cried Israel. "Who's crossin' you?"

"Why, how many tall ships you think I've boarded? And how many shipmates do you think I've seen hanged at Execution Dock?" cried Silver. "It's always because they were in too much of a hurry. You hear me? If you would be smart, and do different, you would be rich. But not you! You'll have your mouthful of rum tomorrow, and go hang later."

"Everybody on old Flint's crew knowed you was all serious, John," said Israel. "They liked to have fun, they did."

"And where are they now?" said Silver. "Pew died a beggar-man. Flint died of rum at Savannah. Ah, they was fun companions! Where are they?"

"But," asked Dick, "when we take over, what do we do with 'em?"

"There's the man for me!" cried the cook admiringly. "All business. Well, what would you think? Maroon 'em ashore, like England done? Cut 'em down in cold blood, like Flint or Billy Bones?"

"Billy would have," said Israel. "'Dead men don't bite,' says he. Well, now Billy don't bite, and he was the roughest hand of all in port."

"Rough and ready," said Silver. "But listen, I'm an easy man—you says I'm all serious, so hear this. Duty is duty, mates. I votes for death. When I'm in Parlyment and riding in my coach, I don't want none of these sea-lawyers showing up. When the time comes, we'll kill 'em!"

"John," cries the coxswain, "you're a man!"

"You'll say so, Israel, when you see," said Silver. "I claim only one thing—I claim Trelawney. I'll wring his calf's head off his body!" he added. "Dick, be a good lad, jump up and get me an apple."

Imagine my terror! I would have leaped out and run for it, but my limbs and heart failed me. I heard Dick begin to rise, and then someone seemed to stop him. Hands exclaimed, "Oh, stow that! Apples is bilge compared to rum, John. Let's have a cup."

"Dick," said Silver, "I trust you. There's the key; you fill a cup, and bring it."

Now I knew, even in my terror, how Mr.

Arrow got the drinks that destroyed him.

During Dick's short absence, Israel spoke quietly in the cook's ear. I could catch only a word or two, but I got some important news: "Not another man of them'll join." So there were still faithful men onboard.

When Dick returned, one after another of the trio took the cup and drank. They toasted luck, old Flint, gold, good food, and themselves.

Just then a brightness fell upon me. I looked up to see the moon shining white on the foresail; and almost at the same time the voice of the lookout shouted, "Land ho!"

CHAPTER 12

COUNCIL OF WAR

With so many feet rushing across the deck, I saw my chance. I slipped out of the barrel, dove behind the foresail, then doubled back toward the stern just in time to join Hunter and Dr. Livesey. All hands gathered on the bow, gazing into the moonlit night. It was like a dream to me, still terrified by what I had heard.

Southwest of us were two low hills a couple of miles apart. Behind was a third and higher one, its summit hidden in a cloud. Then I heard Captain Smollett issuing orders, and the *Hispaniola* altered course slightly to pass east of the island.

"Men, has any one of you ever seen that land?" asked the captain.

"I have, sir," said Silver. "I've watered there with a trader I was cook in."

"The anchorage is on the south, behind an islet?" asked the captain.

"Yes, sir; Skeleton Island they calls it. It were a place for pirates once, and one of my shipmates knowed all their names for it. That hill to the north they calls the Fore-mast Hill; the three hills in a row running southward are called Fore, Main, and Mizzen, sir. The Main—the big 'un in the cloud—they usually calls the Spyglass. They kept lookout there when they was anchored here for cleaning off barnacles, sir."

"I have a chart here," said Captain Smollett. "See if that's the place."

Long John's eyes lit up as he took the chart, but by the fresh look of the paper I knew he would be disappointed. This copy of Billy Bones's map lacked the red crosses and written notes. Silver was clever enough to hide his annoyance.

"Yes, sir," said he, "this is the spot, and well drawed. Aye, here it is: 'Captain Kidd's Anchorage,' as my shipmate called it. A strong current runs along the south, and then away north up the west coast. Right you was, sir," he said, "to cut east of the island. If you was intending to beach and clean the hull, there ain't no better place in these waters."

"Thank you, my man," said Captain Smollett. "I'll ask you later to help us. You may go."

I was surprised at how readily John admitted knowledge of the island. When I saw him drawing near me, I wanted to shudder.

"Ah," he said, "this here island is a sweet spot

for a lad to get ashore on. You'll swim, and climb trees, and hunt goats; and you'll go aloft on them hills like a goat yourself. Why, it makes me almost forget my timber leg. When you want to go exploring, you just ask old John, and he'll put up a snack for you to take along." He gave me a friendly clap on the shoulder and hobbled below.

Captain Smollett was talking with the squire and Dr. Livesey on the quarterdeck. I was trying to think of some excuse to openly interrupt my elders when Dr. Livesey happened to call me over. He wanted me to go below and fetch his pipe. As soon as I was near enough not to be overheard, I said: "Doctor, let me speak. Get the captain and squire down to the cabin, and then make some excuse to send for me. I have terrible news."

The doctor gave a brief start, then recovered. "Thank you, Jim," said he quite loudly, "that was all I wanted to know," as if he had asked me a question. He turned and rejoined the other two.

They spoke together for a bit, and though none gave any sign, Dr. Livesey had plainly conveyed my request. The captain next gave an order to Job Anderson, and he piped the signal that called all hands on deck. The men assembled.

"Men," said Captain Smollett, "this is our destination. Mr. Trelawney has asked for my opinion, and I was able to tell him that every man has done his duty as well as I could wish. This deserves celebration. Therefore, he and I and the doctor are going to the cabin to drink to your health and luck. Rum will be served to you to drink our own, if you wish. I think this a handsome gesture, and if you agree with me, give a good sea-cheer for the squire!"

They did, so fully and heartily that I could hardly believe these same men were plotting for our blood.

"One more cheer for Cap'n Smollett," cried Long John, and this too was given with spirit. The three gentlemen went below, and not long after, the word came that Jim Hawkins was wanted in the cabin.

I found all three seated round the table, a bottle of Spanish wine and some raisins before them. The doctor was smoking away, with his wig on his lap—a sure sign of agitation. The moon shone through the open stern window.

"Now, Hawkins," said the squire, "you have something to say. Speak up."

I told all the details of Silver's conversation as quickly as I could. Nobody interrupted me, nor even moved; they listened intently.

"Jim," said Dr. Livesey, "take a seat." They made me sit down, poured me a glass of wine, and gave me raisins. Each man bowed and drank my good health, praising my service, luck, and courage.

"Now, captain," said the squire, "you were right, and I was wrong. I am a fool, and I await your orders."

"No more a fool than I, sir," returned the captain. "Mutinous crews normally give many signs in advance. I don't know what to think."

"Captain," said the doctor, "Silver is a very remarkable man."

"He'd look remarkably well hanging from a yardarm, sir," returned the captain. "But talk is only talk. I see three or four points. With Mr. Trelawney's permission?"

"You, sir, are the captain. By all means speak," said Mr. Trelawney grandly.

"First point," began Mr. Smollett. "We cannot turn back; they would mutiny at once. Second, we have time yet—at least until this treasure's found. Third point, there are faithful hands. Lastly, it's got to come to blows sooner or later. I propose to take matters in our hands and attack when they least expect it. I assume we can count on your own home servants, Mr. Trelawney?"

"As upon myself," declared the squire.

"Three," reckoned the captain; "ourselves make seven, counting Hawkins here. Now, about the honest crewmen?"

"Most likely Trelawney's own men," said the doctor, "those he had hired before he lit on Silver."

"No," replied the squire. "Coxswain Hands was one of mine. They may be corrupted."

"I thought I could trust Hands," added the captain.

"And to think that they're all Englishmen!" broke out the squire. "Sir, I wish I could simply blow the ship up."

"Well, gentlemen," said the captain, "we must wait, maddening as it may be, and keep a good lookout. I would rather have it over with, but until we know our men that would be reckless. I advise that we watch and wait."

"Jim here," said the doctor, "can help us more than anyone. The men are not shy with him, and Jim is a noticing lad."

"Hawkins, I put great faith in you," added the squire.

I began to feel pretty desperate and helpless, yet circumstances had given me a key role in our safety. In the meantime, talk as we pleased, we could rely on only seven out of the twenty-six. One of these seven was a boy, making the grown men on our side six to their nineteen.

TREASURE ISLAND

PART 3

MY SHORE
ADVENTURE

CHAPTER 13

How My Shore Adventure began

When I came on deck the next morning, the view was completely different. We now lay becalmed about half a mile southeast of the eastern coast. Most of the island was covered with grayish trees, streaks of yellow sand, and clumps of tall pines. Strangely shaped spires of naked rock protruded here and there. The Spyglass was easily the tallest hill on the island, with very steep slopes leading to a flat top. I do not know exactly why, but my heart sank. From the first look, I hated the sight of Treasure Island.

We had a dreary morning's work before us. With no wind, boats had to be lowered and manned in order to tow the ship to the anchorage near Skeleton Island. I volunteered for one of the boats, though I could do nothing useful there.

The men grumbled fiercely in the sweltering

heat. Anderson, in command of my boat, grumbled as loud as anyone. "Well," he said with an oath, "it's not forever." This failing discipline seemed a very bad sign. Until we sighted the island, the men had done their work briskly and willingly.

Long John guided Anderson in steering the ship, for he knew the passage like the palm of his hand. A man in the bow was testing the sea-depth at regular intervals with a piece of lead on a rope, calling out the results as he reeled in the weight. Every spot was deeper than the chart said, but this inaccuracy did not worry John.

"When the tide goes out," he said, "it digs this here passage out like a shovel. I'm not surprised it's deeper now."

We halted between the mainland and Skeleton Island, about a third of a mile from each shore. The splash of our anchor briefly shattered the calm, sending clouds of birds scattering with loud cries. They returned in less than a minute, and all was again silent.

The harbor was a good one, well sheltered by a crescent of forested hills. Less attractive were two swampy, poisonous-looking little rivers emptying into the harbor. We could see no hint of any house or stockade. If it hadn't been for the chart, we might have thought ourselves the first ever to anchor there.

There was still no wind, nor any sound but the

surf booming half a mile away against the beaches
and rocks. The air smelt stagnant, like wet leaves
and rotting tree trunks. The doctor sniffed disap-
provingly. "I don't know about treasure," he said,
"but I'll bet my wig there's fever here."

The men's alarming conduct in the boat got
worse when they returned to the ship. They loafed
around the deck, complaining, obeying resentful-
ly. It seemed even the honest hands had caught the
infection, for no man corrected another. Mutiny
hung over us like a thundercloud.

Long John sensed the trouble too. He bustled
cheerfully from group to group, giving good
advice and setting the example. If an order were
given, John was on his crutch in an instant, with
the cheeriest "Aye, aye, sir!" in the world. When
there was nothing else to do, he sang, almost as if
to hide the discontent. Of all the gloomy features
of that afternoon, this obvious anxiety on Long
John's part made me most nervous of all.

We held a council in the cabin.

"Sir," said the captain, "if I risk another order,
the whole ship'll be at our throats. I am getting
rough, surly answers. If I reply as I should, there
will be battle; if I don't, Silver will see that we're
onto them, and the game's up. We've only one
man to rely on."

"Who is that, captain?" asked the squire.

"Silver, sir. He's as anxious as we are to calm
things down. He'll talk 'em out of it if he gets the

chance, so let's allow the men an afternoon ashore. If they all go, we hold the ship. If none of them go, then we'll hold the cabin, and may God defend the side of right. If some go, you mark my words, sir: Silver'll bring 'em aboard again as mild as lambs."

It was decided. Loaded pistols were issued to all the sure men. Hunter, Joyce, and Redruth were taken into our confidence. They were less surprised at the news than we had expected. The captain went on deck and addressed the crew.

"My lads," said he, "we've had a hot morning's work. A trip ashore'll be refreshing—the boats are still in the water, and any man who pleases may go ashore for the afternoon. I'll fire a gun half an hour before sundown to recall you."

The silly fellows acted as though they would trip over treasure as soon as they landed, for they came out of their sulk immediately. Their cheer echoed off a faraway hill and sent the birds flying and squalling around the anchorage.

The captain was smart enough not to supervise, leaving Silver to arrange the party. Had he remained on deck, he could no longer have pretended ignorance. Silver had a mighty rebellious crew, though I was soon to learn that some hands remained honest. Most likely the crew followed the ringleader's surly example, but only so far. Many men might shirk their work, but few will dare turn pirates and murderers. Shirking cannot get a man hanged, but piracy and murder can.

At last Silver's party of thirteen was ready. Six fellows were to stay onboard, and I got the first of the wild notions that did so much to save our lives. Having left six men behind, Silver could not possibly capture the ship. Those six also could not capture it alone. Since the cabin party had no need of my help, I got the idea to go ashore. I slipped over the side to curl up in the bow of the nearest boat just as it shoved off.

No one paid me any attention, except for the man rowing in the bow, saying, "Is that you, Jim? Keep your head down." But Silver, from the other boat, looked sharply over and called out to know if that were me. I began to regret my impulse.

The crews raced each other for the beach, but my boat won by a hundred yards. When our bow struck among the shoreside trees, Silver and the rest were still far behind. Before anyone could act,

I caught a branch and swung ashore to plunge into the thicket.

"Jim, Jim!" I heard Silver shouting.

As you might guess, I ignored him. Jumping, ducking, and breaking through, I ran until I could run no longer.

CHAPTER 14

The First Blow

I was quite pleased with myself at giving Long John the slip, and now I looked around at this strange land with interest. I had crossed a marshy jungle into a sandy, hilly area maybe a mile long, dotted with a few pines and a lot of twisted trees. On the far side was one of the hills, its two craggy peaks shining vividly in the sun.

This was my first taste of the joy of exploration. I had left my shipmates behind. Before me were only birds and animals. I wandered through the trees, looking at strange new flowers. Here and there I saw snakes. One raised his head from a ledge of rock and hissed at me.

Then I came to a long thicket of small oak-like trees with twisted branches and compact foliage. The woods stretched down from the top of a sandy hill down to the edge of the swamp. One of the little rivers oozed through this swamp on its way to the anchorage. The marsh steamed in the sun, and the outline of the Spyglass trembled through the haze.

All at once there was a rustling in the marsh. Wild ducks quacked and took flight, and soon a great cloud of birds hung screaming and circling. I suspected that some of my shipmates must be approaching, and soon I heard the tones of a human voice not far away. I crawled under cover of the nearest oak to listen, silent as a mouse in my terror.

Another voice answered, and then the first voice—I recognized it as Silver's—continued with what sounded like a story. The other rarely interrupted. I could make out no words, but they spoke in urgent, fierce tones. After a time they seemed to have halted; their voices stopped getting louder, and the birds began to settle down again.

I began to feel that I was neglecting my duty. Having been so foolhardy as to come ashore with these desperadoes, I ought to eavesdrop. I could tell their direction pretty well, both from their voices and the behavior of the few birds still hovering in alarm over one spot. I crawled steadily toward them.

Soon I came to a little, green, wooded valley beside the marsh. Here Long John Silver spoke face to face with another crewman. The sun beat down on them, and Silver had thrown his hat on the ground. He was making an earnest appeal.

"Mate," he was saying, "it's because I thinks the world of you! If I didn't, do you think I'd be here a-warning you? I'm a-speaking to save your neck, Tom; if one of the wild 'uns knew it, what'd become of me?"

"Silver," said the other man, all red in the face, with his voice shaky and hoarse, "you're old, and you're known as honest. You've got money, which lots of poor sailors hasn't. And you're brave. Will you let yourself be led astray by a band of swabs? By God, I'd sooner lose my hand than turn agin my duty—"

He was interrupted by a sudden noise. I had found one of the honest hands. Now, from over the marsh, came news of another: a cry of anger, then another, then one long, horrid scream echoing off the rocks of the Spyglass. The whole flock of birds rose all at once with a whir and a squawk. Then that death-yell faded, and the only sounds were the distant crash of the surf and the rustle of the birds settling back into the marsh.

Tom had leaped at the sound, but Silver had not winked an eye. He stood where he was, resting lightly on his crutch, watching his companion like a coiled snake.

"John!" said the sailor, stretching out his hand.

"Hands off!" cried Silver, leaping back a yard with the sure speed of a trained gymnast. Silver really was a wonder.

"Hands off, if you like, John Silver," said the other. "It's a bad conscience that can make you fear me. But in heaven's name, what was that yell?"

"That?" returned Silver, smiling but warier than ever, his eye gleaming like a crumb of glass. "That? Oh, I reckon that'll be Alan."

At this point Tom was a hero.

"Alan!" he cried. "Then rest his soul for a true seaman! As for you, John Silver, you've long been a mate of mine, but no more. If I die like a dog, I'll die in my duty. You've killed Alan, have you? Kill me too, if you can—but I defies you."

With that, this brave fellow turned his back and walked toward the beach. He did not get far. With a cry John grasped a tree for balance, whipped the crutch upward, and threw it like a spear. It hit poor Tom with stunning violence, point first between the shoulders. His hands flew up; he gasped and then fell.

I will never know how badly Tom was injured, for he got no time to recover. Silver, agile as a monkey even without leg or crutch, was on the top of him next moment and buried his knife twice up to the hilt in that defenseless back. I could hear him pant aloud as he struck the blows.

For the next little while the whole world swam away from before me in a whirling mist—Silver and the birds, and the tall Spyglass hilltop, going round and round and topsy-turvy before my eyes, bells and distant voices ringing in my ear. When I recovered the monster was wiping his bloody knife on the grass, his hat and crutch back in place. Tom lay motionless on the grass in front of him. Nothing else had changed. The sun still shone down with as little mercy as Silver. I could hardly believe I had just witnessed murder.

John put his hand into his pocket, brought out a whistle, and blew it several times. I could not tell what it meant—probably a summons—but it scared me. I might be discovered. They had already slain two of the honest people; why not me next?

Instantly I began to crawl back again, as swiftly and silently as I could, to the more open portion of the wood. Behind me I could hear shouts coming and going between the old pirate and his comrades. As soon as I was clear of the thicket, I ran as I never ran before, caring only to get away from the murderers. I considered myself doomed.

Indeed, how could I be worse off? When the gun fired, what was I to do—go down to the boats with the murderers? Surely the first one to see me would wring my neck. My absence would be proof of my fatal knowledge. I thought it was all over. Good-bye to the *Hispaniola*; good-bye to the squire, the doctor, and the captain! There was nothing left for me but death—either by starvation or the hands of the mutineers.

I was still running all this while, and without realizing it, I had come near the foot of the little hill with the two peaks. Here the oaks grew further apart, less like shrubs and more like trees. There were also a few pines. The air smelled less stagnant than down beside the marsh.

A fresh alarm brought me to a standstill with a thumping heart.

CHAPTER 15

THE MAN
OF THE ISLAND

As I halted at the steep, stony hillside, a bit of gravel rattled downhill toward me. I looked up to see a dark, shaggy figure leap quickly behind a tree-trunk. I couldn't tell whether it was human or animal, only that it was in my path. Suddenly I preferred the danger I knew, so I turned back toward Silver and the boats. The figure began circling around to head me off, flitting from tree-trunk to tree-trunk, too swiftly for me to escape. It was stooped over as it ran. But it moved on two legs and clearly was a man.

I began to recall tales of cannibals. I nearly called for help, then hesitated. He did indeed look human. I remembered my fear of Silver and halted, trying to think of a way to escape. Then I remembered my pistol. My courage returned, and I walked directly toward this man of the island.

He was hiding behind a tree, but as soon as I started toward him he took a step to meet me. He hesitated, drew back, then came forward again. At last, to my wonder and confusion, the hairy creature fell to his knees and held out his clasped hands as if to beg.

"Who are you?" I asked.

"Ben Gunn," he answered in a voice like a rusty lock. "I haven't spoke with an Englishman for three years."

He was very deeply tanned and his dark sunburned skin contrasted with his light eyes. In spite of his startling appearance, he had a handsome face. He dressed worse than a beggar, wearing old tatters of sea-cloth and goatskin held together in makeshift ways. About his waist was an old brass-buckled leather belt.

"Three years!" I cried. "Were you shipwrecked?"

"Nay, mate," he said; "marooned."

I had heard of this horrible pirate punishment. It consisted of abandoning someone on a desolate island with only a pistol and a little ammunition.

"Marooned three years ago," he continued, "and lived on goats and berries and oysters. But, mate, my heart is sore for English diet—cheese especially. You mightn't happen to have any? No? Well, I've spent many a long night dreaming of cheese." He had begun to touch my clothes and boots, investigating me like a wondering child.

"If I can ever get aboard again," said I, "you shall have all the cheese you like."

He perked up. "If ever you can get aboard again, says you?" he repeated. "Why, now, who's to hinder you?"

"Not you," was my reply.

"Right you is," he cried. "What do you call yourself, mate?"

"Jim," I told him.

"Jim, Jim," he said, sounding pleased. "Well now, Jim, I've lived so rough you'd be ashamed to hear of it. To look at me, you wouldn't think I had a religious mother, would you now?" he asked.

"Why, not in particular," I answered.

"Ah, well," he said, "but I had. I could rattle off my catechism so fast you couldn't tell one word from another. And Jim, my downfall begun playing little-boy pranks! My Godly mother predicted I'd end up bad, she did! But Heaven put me here, gave me time to think on it all, and I've sworn off my bad ways. You don't catch me tasting rum much, just a thimbleful now and then. I'm reformed. And, Jim"—looking around and lowering his voice to a whisper—"I'm rich."

Rich, perhaps; insane, certainly. My face must have shown this, for he repeated the statement forcefully: "Rich! And I'll make a rich man of you, Jim. You'll be glad you was the first to find me!"

Then a shadow fell over his face. He grabbed my wrist tightly and, with his other hand, raised a forefinger threateningly before my eyes.

"Now, Jim, tell me the truth. Ain't that Flint's ship?" he asked.

I made an impulsive decision to trust him. "It's not Flint's ship, and Flint is dead. Unfortunately, there are some of Flint's hands aboard."

"Not a man—with one—leg?" he gasped.

"Silver?" I asked.

"Ah, Silver!" he said. "That were his name."

"He's the cook, and the ringleader too."

He was still holding me by the wrist, too

tightly. "If you was sent by Long John," he said, "I'm as good as dead. But where do you suppose you is?"

If he feared Silver, my impulse had been right. I told him the whole story. He listened with keen interest, and when I finished he patted me on the head.

"You're a good lad, Jim," he said; "and you're in a bind, ain't you? Well, just trust Ben Gunn to help you. But Jim, let me ask. Would you call your squire a generous man, especially to them who helped him in a tight spot?"

"The most generous of men," I said without hesitation.

"Aye, but you see," returned Ben Gunn, "I didn't mean giving me a house and clothes and such, Jim, that's not my way. What I mean is, would he be likely to spare me, say, one thousand pounds out of a fortune that's as good as his already?"

"I am sure he would," I said. "All hands were to share in the rewards."

"And would he take me home?" he added, as if bargaining hard.

"Why, the squire's a gentleman," I cried. "And besides, if we got rid of the bad hands, we'd need help to sail the vessel home."

"Ah," he said, "so you would." He seemed very much relieved.

"Now, I'll tell you something, but no more,"

he went on. "I were in Flint's ship when he buried the treasure, he and six strong seamen. They was ashore nearly a week, us staying on the old *Walrus*. One fine day we heard the signal, and here come Flint by himself in a little boat. The six was all dead and buried, mind you, and Flint was all white in the face. How he done it none of us knew—battle, murder, and sudden death, surely. Billy Bones was the mate; Long John was quartermaster. They asked him where the treasure was. 'Ah,' says Flint, 'you can go ashore, if you like, and stay,' he says; 'but as for the ship, she's going after more, by thunder!' That's what he said, long ago.

"Well, I was in another ship three years back, and we sighted this island. 'Boys,' said I, 'here's Flint's treasure; let's land and find it.' The cap'n was displeased, but my messmates and me all landed. Twelve days we looked, and each day they spoke harsher to me. One fine morning all hands went back aboard. 'As for you, Benjamin Gunn,' says they, 'here's a musket and a pick and shovel. Stay and find Flint's money for yourself,' they says.

"Well, Jim, since that day I haven't had a bit of English food. But look at me. Do I look like an ordinary deckhand? I weren't, neither."

He winked and pinched me hard.

"When you speak to your squire, Jim, say just that: 'He weren't, neither.' And tell him this: 'Three years he were the man of this island, rain or shine, and sometimes he would pray, and hope his old mother be alive; but most of Gunn's time was took up with another matter.' Then you'll give him a little pinch, like this."

He pinched me again, as if telling a secret. I tried and failed to imagine myself reciting all this, much less pinching the squire.

"Then," he continued, "you'll say this: 'Gunn is a good man, and he puts a lot more confidence'—say just that!—'in a gen'leman born than in these gen'lemen of fortune, having been one hisself.' "

"Well," I said, "I don't understand one word that you've been saying. But that's neither here nor there; for how am I to get on board?"

"Ah," said he, "that's the hitch. Well, I built a boat, which I keep hid. Worse comes to worse, we might try that after dark. Hi!" he broke out. "What's that?"

Just then the island echoed with the thunder of a cannon. It was at least an hour or two before sunset.

"They have begun to fight!" I cried. "Follow me."

I began to run toward the anchorage, my terrors all forgotten, Ben Gunn trotting close at my side.

"Left, left," he said; "keep to your left hand, mate Jim! Under the trees with you! There's where I killed my first goat. Goats don't come down here now; they fear Benjamin Gunn. Ah!

And there's the cemetery, where I come and prayed when I thought it was Sunday."

He kept talking thus as I ran, not minding that I did not answer. We heard a volley of small-arms fire, then another pause, then a strange sight.

Less than a quarter of a mile ahead, I saw the British flag fluttering in the air above the trees.

TREASURE ISLAND

PART 4

THE STOCKADE

CHAPTER 16

How the Ship
Was Abandoned

Narrative Continued by the Doctor

Silver and his loyal men took the boats ashore at about half past one. The captain, the squire, and I discussed matters in the cabin. There was no wind, or else we would have overwhelmed the six remaining mutineers and headed out to sea. Worse still, Hunter informed us that Jim Hawkins had gone ashore with the rest.

We were sure of Jim's loyalty, but not his safety. We went on deck, and I smelled again the swampy, sickly odor of the anchorage. The six scoundrels sat grumbling under a sail in the forecastle. Both of Silver's boats were tied up near the mouth of the river. Each was guarded by a mutineer.

We decided that Hunter and I should go ashore in the small jollyboat to investigate. The mutineers' boats had gone to the right, but I steered straight in, aiming for the stockade marked on the chart. The boat-guards took immediate notice, and I could see them discussing what to do. Had they run to tell Silver, things might have turned out differently, but they stayed put—perhaps those were their orders. I steered around a slight bend in the coast to land out of their sight. Leaving Hunter to guard the boat, I drew two loaded pistols and ran.

I found the stockade less than a hundred yards away, and it was an excellent defensive position. It was a strong log house on a small hill, large enough to shelter forty men and with holes to shoot from. The area around it was clear of brush and trees, leaving clear lines of fire. The fence was of sharp poles six feet high, with no gate; while trying to destroy or climb over it, attackers could be shot to pieces. Inside the log house was a spring of clear water. With a sharp watch and enough food, a force inside the stockade might hold off a regiment.

I was especially interested in the spring. Our cabin in the *Hispaniola* was comfortable and well stocked with arms, ammunition, food, and even excellent wines. But it lacked abundant fresh water. I was thinking about this when a cry rang across the island. I recognized it from my wartime service. It was the sound of a dying man.

My first thought was that we had lost Jim Hawkins. Not wasting any time, I returned to the shore and jumped back into the jollyboat.

Hunter rowed us swiftly back to the schooner. I found the loyal men shaken by the cry, as was only natural. The squire was sitting down, white as a sheet at the thought of the harm he had led us into. One of the six forecastle hands also looked distraught.

"That man," said Captain Smollett, nodding toward him, "is new to this work. He nearly fainted, doctor, when he heard the cry. If we were to steer him right, he would join us."

We put old Redruth in the gallery between the cabin and the forecastle, with three or four loaded muskets and a mattress for protection. Hunter brought the jollyboat around under the stern entry-port, and Joyce and I set to work loading her with powder tins, muskets, bags of biscuits, kegs of pork, a cask of brandy, and my medicine chest.

In the meantime, the squire and the captain stayed on deck. Smollett hailed the coxswain, the leader of the six forecastle hands left aboard.

"Mr. Hands," he said, "there are two of us with two pistols each. We will shoot any man who signals the shore."

They were taken by surprise. After a little discussion they all tumbled down into the forecastle, thinking no doubt to travel under and attack us from behind. They found Redruth waiting for them below decks, though, and went back. A head peered out on deck.

"Down, dog!" cried the captain.

The head popped back again. For the moment, we heard no more from these faint-hearted seamen. By this time we had the jollyboat as heavily loaded as we dared. Joyce and I boarded through the stern-port, and we made for shore again as fast as Hunter and Joyce could row us.

This second trip definitely got the boat-guards' attention. Just before we lost sight of them around the little point, one jumped ashore and ran inland. I had half a mind to alter my plan and destroy their boats, but if that Silver and the others happened to be near, that could lead to disaster. I took the safer course.

Landing in the same place as before, we set about provisioning the blockhouse. All three of us made the first journey, heavily loaded, tossing our supplies over the wall of the stockade. We posted Joyce at the stockade with six loaded muskets while Hunter and I made another trip back to the jollyboat. In this way we worked until the whole cargo was safe inside the blockhouse. I left Hunter and Joyce to defend the enclosure, and with all my power I rowed back to the *Hispaniola*.

We risked a second boatload, which might seem more daring than it really was. The mutineers outnumbered us, of course, but they were outgunned. They lacked muskets, so we had the advantage of range. We might kill half a dozen before they could even get into pistol-range.

The squire was waiting for me at the stern window, having gotten over his reaction to the death-cry, and we all set to work loading the boat with pork, powder, and biscuit. We packed a musket and a cutlass apiece for the squire, myself, Redruth and the captain. The rest of the arms and powder we dropped overboard in fifteen feet of water. It came to rest on the clean, sandy bottom, bright steel shining in the sunlight.

By this time the tide was going out, and the ship was swinging around on her anchor cable. We heard faint voices ashore hailing the mutineers' boats. This reassured us of the safety of Joyce and Hunter, who were well to the east. But it warned us to get going.

Redruth retreated from his place in the gallery and dropped into the boat, which we then brought around to the side. Captain Smollett reboarded the *Hispaniola*.

"Now, men," said he, "do you hear me?"

There was no answer from the forecastle.

"I am speaking to you, Abraham Gray."

Still no reply.

"Gray," resumed Mr. Smollett, a little louder, "I am leaving this ship, and I order you to follow your captain. I know you are a good man at heart, and I doubt any of you are as bad as you seem. You have thirty seconds to join me."

There was a pause.

"Come, my fine fellow," continued the captain; "don't delay. I'm risking my life and the lives of these gentlemen every second."

There was a sudden scuffle, a sound of blows, and out burst Abraham Gray with a knife-cut on the side of the cheek. He came running to the captain like a dog to the whistle.

"I'm with you, sir," said he. In the next moment he and the captain dropped into the jolly-boat. We shoved off, for we could not be safe until we got inside the stockade.

CHAPTER 17

THE JOLLYBOAT'S
LAST TRIP

NARRATIVE CONTINUED BY THE DOCTOR

This fifth and last trip was the hardest, for our little boat was dangerously overloaded. She was never meant to carry five grown men in the first place, and we also had the powder, pork, and bread-bags. We were in danger of being swamped. I sat in the stern, steering, my clothes soaked by waves lapping over the side.

Worse still, we were in an area where the tide made a strong current westward toward the pirates' boats. "I cannot keep her headed for the stockade, sir," said I to the captain. He and Redruth were at the oars. "The tide keeps washing her down. Could you row a little stronger?"

"Not without swamping the boat," he said. "You must do your best, sir—try to steer so that we gain against the current."

I experimented, but no matter what I did, the

tide kept sweeping us westward. "We'll never get ashore at this rate," I said.

"Even so, we must battle it," replied the captain. "If we slip downwind, we might be boarded by the pirates. However, if we continue as we are, the current must slacken at some point, and then we can dodge back along the shore."

"The current's less a'ready, sir," said Gray, who was sitting in the bow. "You can ease her off a bit."

"Thank you, my man," I said, as if he had always been loyal, for we had all quietly decided to treat him like one of ourselves. Suddenly the captain spoke up again, with urgency in his voice.

"The gun!" he said.

"I have thought of that," I said, for I was sure he was thinking they would blast the fort with it. "They could never get the gun ashore. Even if they did, they could never haul it through the woods."

"Look astern, doctor," replied the captain.

We had entirely forgotten the long nine-pound swivel gun. To our horror, the five rogues were busy getting her ready. The round-shot and powder for the gun had been left behind. The mutineers had easily broken into the place they were stored.

"Israel was Flint's gunner," said Gray hoarsely.

At any rate, we steered directly for the landing place. By this time we had escaped the bad current and were making good time even at the gentle pace we had to row. Unfortunately, this also turned us broadside to the *Hispaniola*, making us a fatter target.

I could hear and see that brandy-faced rascal Israel Hands setting a cannonball down on the deck.

"Who's the best shot?" asked the captain.

"Mr. Trelawney, far and away," I said.

"Mr. Trelawney, will you please pick me off one of these men, sir? Get Hands, if possible," said the captain.

Trelawney was as cool as steel. He loaded and primed his gun with care.

"Now," cried the captain, "easy with that gun, sir, or you'll swamp the boat. All hands stand by to shift position as necessary."

The squire raised his gun, the rowing ceased, and we leaned over to the other side to keep the balance. It was so well done that we did not take on a drop.

By now they had the cannon swiveled around. Hands, who was at the muzzle with the rammer, was the most exposed. Trelawney fired, and to our misfortune, at that very moment Hands bent downward. The ball whistled over him and hit one of the other four, who fell with a cry of agony.

His scream was echoed by his companions onboard—and by many voices from the shore. I looked and saw the other pirates trooping out from among the trees and tumbling into the boats.

"Here they come, sir," I said.

"Row hard, then," cried the captain. "We mustn't worry about swamping her now. If we can't get ashore, we're finished."

"Only one of the boats is being manned, sir," I added; "the crew of the other is most likely going round by shore to cut us off."

"It'll be a hot trip for them, sir, in this sun," returned the captain. "But I'm more worried about the cannon. At this range, my wife couldn't miss us! Squire, when you see them light the match, tell me and we'll make a sudden stop to spoil their aim."

We were now about thirty or forty strokes from the landing beach, a belt of sand now exposed by the outbound tide. We had got around the point, out of sight of the pirates' boat. Now our attackers had to struggle with the difficult spot of current which had cruelly delayed us. The one source of danger was the cannon.

"If I dared," said the captain, "I'd stop and pick off another man."

Aboard the *Hispaniola* they were wasting no time. They ignored their fallen comrade to finish loading. I could see him trying to crawl away in his agony.

"Ready!" cried the squire.

"Hold!" cried the captain, quick as an echo. He and Redruth suddenly rowed backward with a great heave that sent our stern under water.

The cannon cracked in the same instant. I later learned that this was the cannon shot Jim heard; he had not heard the squire's musket shot. The cannonball missed us, but the sudden shift sent our stern under a wave and sank the jollyboat. The captain and myself were standing up, but the other three were dumped over. They came up drenched and bubbling, all of us in water three feet deep.

We would all reach shore safely. But all our supplies were sunk, and to make things worse, only two of our five muskets were in shape to fire. I had grabbed mine from my knees and instinctively held it over my head. The captain had slung his over his shoulder by the strap, with the firing lock sensibly uppermost. The other three had gone down with the boat.

We could already hear voices drawing near in the woods along the shore. We were in danger of being cut off from the stockade. We were also worried Silver's men might attack the stockade. We knew that Hunter was stouthearted, but Joyce was a valet by trade. He was polite and the perfect man to care for a gentleman's clothes, but not likely to make a good foot soldier.

With all this in our minds, we waded ashore as fast as we could. Lost were the poor jollyboat and a good half of our powder and provisions.

CHAPTER 18

END OF THE
FIRST DAY'S FIGHTING

NARRATIVE CONTINUED BY THE DOCTOR

We hurried through the woods toward the stockade. The voices of the mutineers grew louder. Soon we could hear the men crashing through the brush. I made sure that my musket was ready.

"Captain," I said, "Trelawney is the best shot. Give him your gun; his own is useless."

They exchanged guns. Trelawney checked his weapon's load with the cool silence of a man who has faced battle. Gray was unarmed, so I handed him my cutlass. It did all our hearts good to see him scowl and slash the air.

Another forty yards of running brought us to the south side of the stockade. Almost at the same time, seven mutineers led by boatswain Anderson appeared in the southwestern corner.

We took them by surprise. The squire and I fired, as did Hunter and Joyce from the blockhouse.

It was rather a scattered volley, but one man went down. The rest of the men disappeared into the trees. After reloading, we walked over to check on the fallen enemy. He was stone dead—shot through the heart.

We began to rejoice over our success when a pistol cracked from the bush. A ball whistled close past my ear, and poor Tom Redruth stumbled and fell. Both the squire and I returned fire at the unseen enemy, but we probably only wasted powder. Then we reloaded and turned our attention to poor Tom. I saw immediately that he was in bad shape.

The readiness of our return volley may have inspired the mutineers to give us some room, for we were able to get Tom over the stockade without further threat. We carried him groaning and bleeding into the log-house.

The poor old fellow had been a model of stolid loyalty from the beginning. He had stood fast in the gallery, silently obeyed every order, never complained. He was the oldest of us, and now we had to lay this faithful old servant down to die.

The squire knelt beside him and held his hand, crying like a child.

"Am I going, doctor?" he asked.

"Tom, my man," I said, "you're going home."

"I wish I had had a lick at them with the gun first," he replied.

"Tom," said the squire, "say you forgive me, won't you?"

"Would that be respectful, from me to you, squire?" was the answer. "But yes, sir, I forgive anything there is to forgive."

After a little while of silence, Redruth asked if somebody would read a prayer. "It's the custom, sir," he added apologetically. Those were his final words. He passed away soon after.

In the boat I had noticed that the captain's clothing seemed abnormally bulky. Now he emptied out a great many useful things. They included the British flag, a Bible, a coil of stout rope, a pen, ink, the logbook, and pounds of tobacco. Inside the fence lay a tall fir tree, felled and trimmed, and Smollett and Hunter set it up at one corner of the house for a flagpole. Climbing onto the roof, he ran up the British flag.

This seemed to relieve Smollett mightily. He re-entered the log-house and set about inventorying supplies, but the loss of Tom was still on his mind. As soon as our captain finished, he came forward with another flag and reverently spread it on the body.

"Don't fault yourself, sir," he said, shaking the squire's hand. "He died a loyal hand, doing his duty to captain and squire. He is a man without blame. It may not be exactly what a priest would say, but it's a fact."

Then he pulled me aside.

"Dr. Livesey," he said, "how many weeks before they send a ship from Bristol to look for us?"

I told him it was a question not of weeks but of months. Blandly was to send a ship after us if we were not back by the end of August. "You can calculate for yourself," I said.

"Why, yes," replied the captain, scratching his head. "And it will be close. A pity we lost that second load; we have enough powder and shot, but the rations will be very short. They may be so short, Dr. Livesey, that while we would of course wish Redruth alive again, we may also be glad of one less mouth to feed."

Just then a round-shot roared and whistled high above our roof and plumped far beyond us in the woods.

"Oho!" said the captain. "Blaze away! You've

little enough powder already, my lads."

The second shot was better aimed. The nine-pound ball landed inside the stockade, scattering a cloud of sand but doing no further damage.

"Captain," said the squire, "the house cannot be seen from the ship. They must be aiming at the flag. Wouldn't it be wiser to take it in?"

"Strike my colors?" cried the captain. "Not I, sir!" As soon as he had said the words, I think we all agreed it was a bold gesture. To haul down the flag was the traditional seafaring gesture of surrender; to keep it flying showed our defiance.

All through the evening the mutineers kept thundering away. Ball after ball flew over, or fell short, or kicked up sand in the enclosure. They could do little damage, for the high angle of fire robbed their shots of much force. It was like having round-shot dropped from the sky rather than blasted from a nine-pounder cannon. We soon got used to the bombardment, though the mutineers did manage to drop one ball through our roof. It went right through the floor as well, harming no one.

"There is one good thing about all this," observed the captain. "The woods in front of us are likely clear. The tide has likely uncovered our stores. We need volunteers to go and bring in pork."

Gray and Hunter volunteered and armed themselves. They headed out of the stockade for the beach, but the mutineers had arrived first. Four or five of them were busy loading our stores into a boat commanded by Silver. Every man now had a musket, so they must have smuggled some aboard before we left Bristol. Our men trudged back to report the bad news.

The captain sat down to write his log, and here is the beginning of the entry:

> Alexander Smollett, master; David Livesey, ship's doctor; Abraham Gray, carpenter's mate; John Trelawney, ship's owner; John Hunter and Richard Joyce, landsmen—those of the ship's company that remain faithful—with stores for ten days with rationing. Came ashore this day and flew British colors on the log-house in Treasure Island. Thomas Redruth, landsman, shot by the mutineers; James Hawkins, cabin boy—

At the same time, I was wondering over poor Jim Hawkins' fate. Then came a shout on the landward side.

"Somebody hailing us," said Hunter, who was on guard.

"Doctor! Squire! Captain! Hello, Hunter, is that you?" came the cries.

I ran to the door in time to see Jim Hawkins, safe and sound, climbing over the stockade.

CHAPTER 19

THE GARRISON
IN THE STOCKADE

NARRATIVE RESUMED BY JIM HAWKINS

Ben Gunn halted me when he saw the flag.

"Now," he said, "there's your friends, sure enough."

"More likely it's the mutineers," I answered.

"Silver would fly the Jolly Roger, don't doubt that," he cried. "No, that's your friends. There's been fighting too, and I reckon your friends is winning; and here they are ashore in Flint's old stockade. Flint weren't afraid of none but Silver."

"Maybe so," I said. "I should hurry and join my friends."

"Not yet, mate," returned Ben. "You're a good boy, but on'y a boy. Now, Ben Gunn is sly. I won't come till I see your born gen'leman give his word of honor. Remember I told you to say: 'He puts more confidence in a gen'leman born'—and then pinch him." He pinched me a third time,

130

entirely serious about it all. "Oh! Then you'll say, 'Ben Gunn has his own reasons.'"

"Of course," I said, as if I relayed such messages every day.

"And you know where to find Ben Gunn, Jim—just where you found him today. Whoever comes must come alone, bearing the white flag."

"I believe I understand," I said. "You have a proposal for the squire or the doctor, and you will be where I found you. Is that all?"

"You won't forget?" he inquired anxiously.

"I won't," I said. "And now may I go?"

"I reckon you can, Jim. And, Jim, if you was to see Silver, you wouldn't sell out Ben Gunn? Not for no reason, says you—"

He was interrupted by a loud boom. A cannonball tore through the trees and thumped into sand not a hundred yards from us. Each of us took off running in a different direction. After a time another shot boomed, and another, and so on for a good hour. There seemed no refuge from it, but toward the end I took heart. I dared not yet venture toward the stockade, where most of the balls landed, but I took a long detour eastward and crept down to the shoreside trees.

The sun had just set. The sea breeze was rustling the woods and the water, and the tide had exposed a sandy beach. After the day's heat, the cold air chilled me through my jacket.

The *Hispaniola* still lay at anchor, but sure

enough, she now flew the Jolly Roger—the black flag of piracy. With a flash of red fire and a bang, one final round-shot whistled through the air. The cannonade was over.

After the bombardment I lay for some time watching the bustle. Men with axes were demolishing something on the beach—the poor jolly-boat, I later learned. Away near the river-mouth a great fire was lit, and a boat shuttled between the fire and the ship. The once-sullen men were now shouting and laughing at the oars like children. I had lived in a tavern long enough to hear rum in their voices.

After watching for a while I thought I had best get to the stockade. I was pretty far down on the low, sandy spit that enclosed the anchorage to the east. With the tide out, this narrow point of land joined to Skeleton Island. Some distance down the spit I saw a large white rock rising from low bushes. Might this be the rock where Ben Gunn kept his boat? If I ever needed one, I now had an idea where to look.

I skirted among the woods until I reached the stockade's shoreward side and was soon enjoying a warm welcome from the faithful party. I told the whole story, neglecting to pinch the squire.

When I finished, I had a look about. The house was made entirely of plain pine logs, its floor a foot or more above the sand. One corner had a stone slab for a hearth, with a rusty iron basket to contain the fire. The spring was just outside the front door, enclosed by a porch. A ship's kettle with its bottom knocked out had been sunk into the sand to serve as a basin.

All timber close to the stockade had been cut to build the house and the fence, leaving only stumps. The only plants in the area were some ferns and little bushes where the stream from the spring ran. The forest still flourished high and dense not far from the stockade.

The cold evening breeze whistled through every crevice in the primitive building and sprinkled the floor with a continual rain of fine sand. There was sand in our eyes, our teeth, our suppers, even dancing in the bottom of the spring. Our chimney was a square hole in the roof, and did little good. Much of the smoke remained inside, so we were always coughing and wiping our eyes.

Gray, the new man, had his face bandaged for a cut he had got breaking away from the mutineers. Poor old Tom Redruth lay stiffening along the wall under the flag.

Had we been allowed to sit idle, we would probably have begun to mope, but Captain Smollett would have none of it. All hands were divided into watches. The doctor and Gray and I one group; the squire, Hunter, and Joyce were the other. Two men were sent for firewood and two more to dig a grave. The doctor was named cook; I was put at the door as sentry. The captain himself went from one group to another, keeping up our spirits and helping where needed.

From time to time the doctor came to the door for fresh air. When he did so, he would speak with me.

"That man Smollett," he said once, "is a better man than I, and I do not say that lightly, Jim."

Another time he came and was silent for a while. Then he tilted his head to one side and looked at me. "What sort of man is this Ben Gunn?" he asked.

"I do not know, sir," I said. "But I am not sure he's sane."

"That is no surprise," returned the doctor. "A man who has spent three years alone on a desert island, Jim, can't expect to appear as sane as you or me. Not human nature. Didn't you say he wished for cheese?"

"Yes, sir, cheese," I answered.

"Well, Jim," he said, "see what good comes of having refined tastes in food. You've seen my snuffbox, but you have never seen me use snuff. That is because I keep a piece of Parmesan cheese in it instead of snuff. Well, now Ben Gunn shall have that cheese!"

Before supper we buried old Tom in the sand and stood around his grave with hats off for a while. We had collected much firewood, but not enough to suit the captain, who shook his head and said: "We must do better tomorrow."

When we had eaten our pork and each had a good stiff glass of brandy, the three chiefs gathered in a corner to figure out a plan of action.

They seemed baffled over what to do. The food supply was so low that we could be starved into surrender long before help came. They decided that our best hope was to kill off the pirates until they either struck their colors or ran away with the ship. They were already reduced from nineteen to fifteen, with two more wounded—one perhaps dying. With all due care for our own safety, we were to take every shot at them we could. Besides, we had two allies to help us beat them: rum and swamp fever.

Even at this distance, we could hear evidence of the rum. They roared and sang late into the night. As for the fever, they had camped by the swamp without remedies or doctor. "I'll bet my wig half of them will be sick within a week," said Dr. Livesey. "So, unless we are all shot down somehow, they'll be glad to return to the schooner."

"First ship I ever lost," said Captain Smollett.

I was dead tired, as you may expect. After a great deal of tossing, I slept like a log.

When I woke up to the sound of bustle and voices, the rest had already eaten breakfast and cut a good deal of firewood. "Flag of truce!" I heard someone say; and then, immediately after, with a cry of surprise, "Silver himself!"

I jumped up, rubbed my eyes, and ran to look.

CHAPTER 20

SILVER'S EMBASSY

It was still quite early, and cold enough to chill my bones. The sky was bright and cloudless overhead. Silver and a lieutenant stood outside the stockade, knee-deep in a low white fog. What a damp, feverish, unhealthy place! Silver's lieutenant was waving a white cloth.

"Keep indoors, men. Ten to one this is a trick," said the captain. Then he called out, "Who goes? Stand, or we fire."

"Flag of truce," cried Silver.

Keeping in cover, the captain turned and said to us, "Dr. Livesey, your group has the lookout. Take the north side, if you please. Jim, watch east and Gray, the west. The rest, all hands to load muskets. Lively, men, and careful."

He turned again to the mutineers. "And what do you want with your flag of truce?" he cried.

This time Silver's lieutenant replied.

"Cap'n Silver, sir, to come on board and discuss terms," he shouted.

"Cap'n Silver! Who's he?" cried the captain, adding to himself, "Cap'n, is it? Ha!"

Long John answered for himself. "Me, sir. These poor lads have chosen me cap'n, after your *desertion*, sir. We're willing to come to terms, no bones about it. All I ask is your word, Cap'n Smollett, to let me safe out of this here stockade after we talk, and one minute to get out o' shot before a gun is fired."

"My man," said Captain Smollett, "I have not the slightest desire to talk to you. If you wish to talk to me, come forward. If there's any treachery, it'll be on your side, and the Lord help you."

"That's enough for me, cap'n," shouted Long John cheerily. "I know a gentleman when I meet him."

His lieutenant tried to hold Silver back, but Silver just laughed and advanced to the stockade. He threw over his crutch and then, with amazing skill and strength, climbed safely to the other side.

I admit that I was neglecting my sentry duty. I had already deserted my eastern guard-post and crept up behind the captain, who had sat down in the doorway, whistling "Come, Lasses and Lads." Dr. Livesey had also come over to listen.

Silver had hard work getting up the sandy slope with his crutch, but he stuck to it. At last he arrived before the captain, saluting handsomely.

He was wearing his best blue coat with brass buttons and a fancy hat.

"Here you are, my man," said the captain, raising his head. "You had better sit down."

"You ain't a-going to let me inside, cap'n?" complained Long John. "It's a cold morning, sir, to sit outside upon the sand."

"Why, Silver," said the captain, "if you had remained loyal, you would be sitting in your galley. You're either my ship's cook—and you were treated well—or 'Cap'n Silver,' a mutineer who deserves hanging!"

"Well, well, cap'n," answered the sea cook, sitting down on the sand, "you'll have to give me a hand up again, that's all. A pretty place you have here. Ah, there's Jim! Good morning to you, Jim. Doctor, my regards. Why, there you all are together like a happy family, in a manner of speaking."

"If you have anything to say, my man, say it," said the captain.

"Right you are, Cap'n Smollett," replied Silver. "Duty is duty. Well, that was a good move of yours last night. I don't deny it; some of you are handy with a handspike. I'll admit some of my people was shook up by it; maybe that's why I'm here for terms. But cap'n, I won't come twice, by thunder! We'll have to keep sentry and ease off on the rum. Maybe you think we were all into the rum, but I'll tell you I was sober. I was on'y dog tired; and if I'd awoke a second sooner, I'd 'a caught you, I would. He wasn't dead when I got round to him, not he."

"Well?" said Captain Smollett, coolly. It made no sense to him, but he did not let that show. I suspected Ben Gunn had stepped in. Perhaps he waited until they were all drunk, then bashed someone's head with something heavy, like a ship's handspike or prying-bar. I calculated with glee that our enemies were reduced to fourteen.

"Well, here it is," said Silver. "We want that treasure, and we'll have it! You want to save your lives, I reckon. You have a chart, haven't you?"

"That's as may be," scowled the captain.

"I know you have one," returned Long John impatiently. "Being surly will do you no good, take my word. What I mean is, we want your chart. I never meant you no harm, myself."

"That's false," interrupted the captain. "We know exactly what you meant to do, and we don't care, for now you can't do it." Smollett calmly began to fill a pipe.

"If Abe Gray—" Silver broke out.

"Now just a minute!" cried Mr. Smollett. "Gray told me nothing, and I asked him nothing. I would sooner see you and him and this whole island blown into blazes first. So there."

This little whiff of temper seemed to cool Silver down. "Fair enough," said he. "I would set no limits to what gentlemen might do for honor's sake. And seein' as how you are about to take a pipe, cap'n, I'll feel free to do likewise."

He filled and lit a pipe. The two men sat silently smoking for quite a while, acting unconcerned. I watched in great suspense.

"Now," resumed Silver, "here it is. You give us the chart to get the treasure, and stop shooting poor seamen and bashing in their heads while asleep. You do that, and we'll offer you a choice. Either you come aboard with us, once the treasure is loaded, and then I'll give you my word of honor to put you somewhere safe ashore. Or if you prefer, some of my hands being rough and having bad memories of you, then you can stay here. We'll divide stores with you, man for man. And I'll give my word as before: the first ship I sight, I'll send here to pick you up. Now, that's as fair as you can get. And I hope," he added, raising his voice, "that all hands hear my words, for what is spoke to one is spoke to all."

Captain Smollett rose from his seat and knocked out the ashes of his pipe.

"Is that all?" he asked.

"Every last word, by thunder!" answered John. "Refuse that, and you've seen the last of me but musket-balls."

"Very good," said the captain. "Now you'll hear me. If you'll come up one by one, unarmed, I'll clap you all in irons and take you home to a fair trial in England. If you won't, I promise I'll see you all dead. You can neither find the treasure nor

navigate the ship. You can't fight us; Gray, there, got away from five of you. You're in bad shape, Master Silver, and I'll make it worse, for by heaven, I'll put a bullet in your back when next I meet you. Now get out of here, my lad, and quickly."

Silver's eyes flashed with wrath. He shook the fire out of his pipe.

"Give me a hand up!" he cried.

"Not I," returned the captain.

"Who'll give me a hand up?" he roared.

None of us moved. Swearing and threatening, he crawled along the sand till he got hold of the porch and could hoist himself again upon his crutch. Then he spat into the spring.

"There!" he cried. "That's what I think of ye. Before an hour's out, I'll stove in your old blockhouse like a rum keg. Laugh, by thunder! Before an hour's out, ye'll laugh in hell. Them that die'll be the lucky ones."

With a dreadful oath he stumbled off and ploughed down the sand. His lieutenant helped him across the stockade and they disappeared into the trees.

CHAPTER 21

THE ATTACK

As soon as Silver disappeared, the captain turned around to find only Gray at his post. It was the first time we had ever seen him angry.

"Quarters!" he roared. And then, as we all slunk back to our places, "Gray," he said, "I'll put your name in the log. You've stood by your duty like a seaman. Mr. Trelawney, I'm surprised at you, sir. Doctor, I thought you had worn the King's uniform! Is this how you served at Fontenoy, sir? Why is no one loading the muskets?"

Everyone was red-faced. We of the doctor's watch hurried back to our firing-holes while the rest got busy loading the spare muskets. The captain watched in silence for a time before he spoke.

"My lads," said he, "I've given Silver a good, red-hot broadside—on purpose. Before the hour's out, as he said, we shall be boarded. As you know, we are outnumbered, but we have shelter. A minute ago I would also have said we had discipline. I've no doubt that we can whip them, if you choose." He walked around the interior, looking outward in each direction.

On the two short sides of the house, east and west, there were only two firing-holes; on the south side with the porch, also two; on the north side, five. We seven had twenty muskets. In the middle of each side we had made a neat stack of firewood to form a sort of table to hold four loaded muskets and extra ammunition. In the midst of the blockhouse lay the cutlasses.

"Put out the fire," said the captain. "The chill is past, and we mustn't have smoke in our eyes." Mr. Trelawney did so.

"Hawkins, you have not had breakfast. Eat it at your post," continued Captain Smollett. "Hunter, serve out a round of brandy to all hands."

While this was going on, the captain refined his plan. "Doctor, you will take the door. Watch, but don't expose yourself. Fire through the porch. Hunter, take the east side. Joyce, you stand by the west, my man. Mr. Trelawney, you are the best shot—you and Gray will take this long north side, with the five firing-holes; it is the most dangerous. We cannot have them getting close and using those holes to shoot us like caged rats. Hawkins, neither you nor I are great shots, so we'll stand by to load and give a hand."

By now the bright sun had burned off the low mist. It grew very hot. Jackets and coats were flung aside, shirts opened, sleeves rolled up, and we stood anxiously to our watch.

An hour passed.

"Hang them!" said the captain. "This is dull. Gray, whistle a tune for us."

At that moment came the first news of the attack.

"If you please, sir," said Joyce, "if I see anyone, shall I fire?"

"I told you so!" cried the captain.

"Thank you, sir," answered Joyce with perfect courtesy.

Nothing happened immediately, but we were all on high alert. The captain stood tight-lipped and frowning in the middle.

A few seconds later, Joyce leveled his musket and fired. The *bang!* had scarcely died away before it was answered. From the trees on every side of the stockade came a scattered volley of musket shots, some of which struck the log-house. As the smoke cleared away, the stockade and the woods looked as quiet and empty as before. Our enemies stayed hidden.

"Did you hit your man?" asked the captain.

"I believe not, sir," replied Joyce.

"Good to have the truth, at least," muttered Captain Smollett. "Load his gun, Hawkins. How many were on your side, doctor?"

"Three shots were fired on this side," said Dr. Livesey. "Two close together, one farther to the west."

"Three!" repeated the captain. "And on yours, Mr. Trelawney?"

This answer was less certain, for the squire counted seven but Gray thought he saw eight or nine. Only a single shot each had come from east and west, indicating that the main attack would come from the north. Captain Smollett made no change in his arrangements, but reminded us how important it was to shoot the mutineers as they tried to cross the stockade. If they got up the hill and close to the blockhouse, we would lose the advantage of the building.

We didn't have long to consider. Suddenly and with a cheer, a little cloud of seven pirates leaped from the northern woods and charged the stockade. At the same moment, another ragged volley came from the woods all around. One musket-ball sang through the doorway and smashed the doctor's musket.

The boarders swarmed over the fence like monkeys. The squire and Gray fired again and again; three men fell, one forward into the enclosure, two back on the outside. One of these was evidently more frightened than hurt, for he was on his feet again in a moment and disappeared among the trees.

Two dead, one fled; four safely into the stockade. From the shelter of the woods seven or eight men kept up a steady but harmless fire.

The four who had boarded made straight for the building, cheered on by those in the trees. Both Gray and Mr. Trelawney fired again and missed. In a moment, the four pirates had swarmed up the mound and were upon us.

The head of boatswain Job Anderson appeared at the middle firing-hole. "At 'em, all hands—all hands!" he roared.

At the same moment, another pirate grasped Hunter's musket by the muzzle, wrenched it out through the firing-port, then reversed it, and smashed our man in the head. Hunter fell senseless to the floor. Meanwhile a third ran around the house to the doorway. He raised his cutlass to attack the doctor.

Our position was utterly reversed. One moment we had been firing from cover at an exposed enemy; now our cover was penetrated. The log-house was full of powder-smoke, which helped us. I heard confused cries, the flash and bang of pistol shots, and one loud groan.

"Out, lads, out, and fight 'em in the open! Cutlasses!" cried the captain.

I snatched a cutlass from the pile just as someone else did, and got an accidental cut across the knuckles. I hardly felt it as I dashed out into the clear sunlight. Someone was close behind me. The doctor was chasing his attacker down the hill. He beat down the man's guard, then sent him sprawling on his back with a great slash across the face.

"Round the house, lads! Round the house!" cried the captain, and despite the hurly-burly I sensed a change in his voice. I obeyed and turned eastward to run around the corner of the house. I found myself face to face with Anderson, who roared aloud and raised his cutlass to strike. I leaped aside, lost my footing in the sand, and tumbled head over heels down the slope.

When I had first gone outside, the other mutineers had already been swarming up the stockade to finish us. One man in a red nightcap, with his cutlass in his teeth, had even got a leg over the top. It had all happened so fast that when I got to my feet, he was still up there, with another just showing his head above the stockade.

And yet in this brief moment the fight was over and we had won. Gray, close behind me, cut down Anderson before he could recover from his slash at me. Another had been shot while trying to fire into the blockhouse and now lay in agony, the pistol still smoking in his hand. I had seen the doctor dispose of a third with his cutlass. The last of the four who remained healthy had discarded his cutlass and fled. I saw him clambering back over the stockade.

"Back to our posts and fire from the house!" cried the doctor.

But no more shots were fired. The last boarder successfully escaped into the woods with the rest. In three seconds nothing remained of the attacking party but the five who had fallen, four inside the stockade and one outside.

The doctor and Gray and I hastened inside. The survivors might soon rally and start firing again.

By now the smoke had somewhat cleared out of the house, showing us the price we had paid for victory. Hunter lay stunned at his post; we had no idea how badly he might be hurt. Joyce lay dead from a shot to the head. In the center the squire was supporting the captain, both quite pale.

"The captain's wounded," said Mr. Trelawney.

"Have they run?" asked Mr. Smollett.

"All that could," replied the doctor. "But five of them will never run again."

"Five!" cried the captain. "Much better. Five losses against three leaves us four to their nine. That's better odds than before. We were seven to nineteen then, or thought we were, which is just as bad."

In reality, the mutineers were down to eight. The man shot by Mr. Trelawney from the jollyboat had died that evening, as we learned later.

PART 5

MY SEA ADVENTURE

CHAPTER 22

How My Sea Adventure Began

The mutineers stayed away; as the captain put it, they had "got their rations for the day." We had some peace and quiet to care for the wounded. While the squire and I cooked our lunch outside, we could hear the loud groans of the wounded.

Of the eight men who had fallen in the action, only three still breathed—the pirate who had been shot at the firing-hole, Hunter, and Captain Smollett. The mutineer died in surgery, and Hunter never awoke from the bone-breaking blow he received. Sometime that evening he went quietly off to his Maker.

The captain's wounds were painful but not dangerous. Job Anderson's shot had broken his shoulder blade and touched the lung; a second shot had struck him in the calf. The doctor expected him to recover, but for several weeks he would be hampered. Smollett was not supposed to walk, move his arm, nor even speak if he could help it. My own accidental cut across the knuckles was a fleabite, easily patched by Doctor Livesey.

After lunch, squire, doctor, and captain met for discussion. This lasted until a little past noon, and when it was over the doctor put on his hat. He armed himself with pistols, a cutlass, and a musket. He put the chart in his pocket. Then he climbed over the north side of the stockade and soon vanished into the trees.

Gray and I were sitting together at the far end of the blockhouse so as not to listen in on our officers. When the doctor left, Gray stopped smoking and asked me if Livesey had gone mad.

"I doubt it," I said. "He's about the sanest of us."

"Well, shipmate," said Gray, "he's certainly not acting like a sane man, leaving the stockade like that."

"I think I can guess what he's up to," replied I. "I bet he's going to meet Ben Gunn."

Later I learned I was right. In the meantime, I had another thought that was quite wrong. Sitting in the stiflingly hot house, heat rising from the blistering sand, I began to envy the doctor. He was out walking in the cool shade of the woods while I sat here broiling. My clothes stuck to the sap leaking from the logs. I was surrounded by blood and dead bodies. I felt an overwhelming need to get out. As I washed out the blockhouse and cleaned up after lunch, my disgust and envy grew stronger by the minute.

I found myself next to a bread-bag with no one watching, and I quickly filled both my coat pockets with biscuits. This was the first step toward my next adventure. I admit that I was a fool on a foolish mission, but at least I was a prepared fool. If anything bad should happen, the biscuits would sustain me until well into the next day. I already had a powder horn and bullets, and I next took a pair of pistols. Now I felt well-armed.

At its core, my idea was not a bad one. I planned to go down to the white rock and see if Ben Gunn's boat was there. If I asked permission, surely Smollett and the squire would refuse, so my only option was to sneak out. That, of course, was bad enough to make the whole escapade a wrong behavior. But I was only a boy, and had made up my mind.

A bit later, when the squire and Gray were busy helping the captain with his bandages, I saw my opportunity. I bolted over the stockade into the thicket and was out of earshot before my companions knew it. This was my second and worst misdeed: leaving only two healthy men to guard the house. Like the first, though, it ultimately helped save us all.

I made for the east coast, hoping to evade detection by traveling down the seaward side of the spit. It was late afternoon and still sunny, with a higher sea breeze than usual. The woods continued right up to the beach with its constant wash of foamy breakers. It was blue sea all the way to the horizon. I turned south to walk along the beach, and when I thought I had gone far enough, I took cover in some thick bushes and crept cautiously up to the edge of the spit.

Behind me was the turbulent sea. The anchorage before me was still as a mirror, and fog was setting in. The *Hispaniola* flew the Jolly Roger.

Alongside her lay a boat, and I could recognize Silver in its stern. A couple of men leaned off the *Hispaniola* toward Silver's boat, one with a red cap. He was the same rogue I had seen climbing the stockade a few hours before. I was too far away to hear, but it seemed they were talking and laughing. Then I heard the most horrid, unearthly screaming, which startled me badly until I remembered the voice of Captain Flint, Silver's parrot. I thought I could see her bright plumage perched on his wrist.

Soon after, the boat headed for shore. The man with the red cap and his comrade went below. Meanwhile the sun had gone down behind the Spyglass, and fog was descending fast. If I waited any longer, it would be too dark to find the boat.

I could easily see the white rock perhaps an eighth of a mile further down the spit. I had to crawl among the bushes, which took me until past dark. Right below the rock there was a tiny, well-hidden grassy hollow with a small goatskin tent. I dropped down and lifted the goatskin.

There was Ben Gunn's boat: a small, crude, lopsided framework of tough wood with a goatskin covering. It had a low crosspiece and a double paddle. This sort of boat is called a coracle, and Ben Gunn's boat was like the first, worst coracle ever made by man. It looked as if a grown man's weight would have sunk it. Yet like any coracle, it had the great advantage of being easy to carry.

Having found the coracle, you would have thought I had got into enough mischief for a day, but not me. I liked my next idea so well that I believe I would have carried it out even had Captain Smollett himself personally forbidden me. The mutineers had got a painful lesson that morning, and I was sure they were eager to raise anchor and sail off. I saw no reason to allow this. Since they had failed to provide their watchmen with a boat, I thought I might slip out under cover of darkness and cut the *Hispaniola's* anchor cable. Thus set adrift, she would likely run aground in the night.

I had a hearty meal of biscuits while waiting for full darkness. The heavy night fog was perfect for my purpose. When at last I shouldered the coracle and stumbled out of the hollow, I could see only two points on the anchorage: the great fire ashore, where the defeated pirates lay drinking rum by the swamp, and the reflection of the light from the ship's cabin on the dense fog. The outgoing tide had turned the schooner's bow toward me.

To reach the edge of the water, I had to plod through a long belt of swampy sand. I waded out a little way and set my coracle on the water, keel downward.

CHAPTER 23

THE EBB TIDE RUNS

The lopsided coracle floated well but was awkward to manage. No matter what I did, she mostly turned in circles and drifted with the current. Even Ben Gunn himself has admitted that she was "hard to handle till you knew her way." From what I could tell, 'her way' was to turn in every direction but the one I wanted to go. Had the ebb tide not swept me directly toward the cabin light, I am sure I would never have reached the *Hispaniola*.

Soon a shape darker than the fog loomed over me, and then I could make out her masts and hull. In the very next moment the entire bow was visible and I was passing directly by the *Hispaniola*'s anchor cable.

Without time to think, I made a grab and caught hold of the heavy rope. It was tight as a bowstring. One cut with my sea-knife and the schooner would be washed out with the tide. Then

I remembered hearing that when a tight rope is suddenly cut, it can be as dangerous and unpredictable as a wild horse. It might knock the coracle and me clean out of the water. I hesitated. I could hear loud talking from the ship's cabin, but my mind was on other matters.

Just when I was ready to abandon my idea, fortune favored me. The light wind blowing from the southeast and south had hauled around to blow toward the southwest. While I was pondering, a puff forced the schooner up into the current. I felt the rope slacken in my grasp, and made haste to slice away at its strands. When only two strands remained intact, I halted to await another breath of wind.

With nothing to do but wait, I listened to the

loud voices. The coxswain, Israel Hands, was arguing with my friend in the red nightcap. Both were obviously drunk and getting drunker. One of them opened the stern window, and I heard the *plump* of an empty bottle hitting the sea.

The curses flew like hailstones, but just when the debate seemed about to turn violent, the hubbub died down for a few minutes. It would then start all over again, working its way back up to shouted profanities. My wait was long enough for the two mutineers to complete a few cycles of vulgar argument.

I could see the warm glow of the great campfire ashore. Someone was singing a dull old sailor's song over and over again, one I had often heard on the voyage:

> **"But one man of her crew alive,**
> **What put to sea with seventy-five."**

This seemed woefully fitting after their cruel losses earlier in the day. Indeed, from what I saw, these mutineers were as heartless as the sea they sailed on.

At last the breeze came; the schooner sidled nearer in the dark. I felt the rope slacken once more. With a good effort, I cut through the last tough strands.

Almost instantly, the current swept my little coracle against the *Hispaniola*'s bow. At the same time, the schooner began to spin slowly in place across the current.

I rowed fiercely so that I wouldn't be swamped, but I found I could not push the coracle directly off. Instead I began to shove sternward, and after some hard effort I was clear of my dangerous neighbor. Just as I gave the last push, my hands came across a light cord trailing overboard from the stern. I cannot say why I did this, but I caught it with a quick grab and pulled. It was tight, strong enough to hold me.

I grew curious. I decided to pull myself up and have a look through the cabin window.

When I thought I was near enough, I peeped inside the cabin. By this time the schooner and my little boat were gliding pretty swiftly through the water. Indeed, we had already come level with the campfire. One glance inside told me why Hands and his companion had not noticed the schooner's drift. They were locked in a deadly wrestle, trying to strangle one another.

I dropped back onto the coracle's crosspiece just before it drifted out from under me. In my mind I could still see those two furious faces swaying under the smoky lamp. The cabin light had ruined my night vision, and I shut my eyes to hasten its return.

By the campfire, the endless ballad had finally given way to the familiar chorus:

"Fifteen men on the dead man's chest—
Yo-ho-ho, and a bottle of rum!
Drink and the devil had done for the rest—
Yo-ho-ho, and a bottle of rum!"

Drink and the devil were hard at work in the schooner's cabin, I thought. Then the coracle lurched suddenly, changed course, and speeded up. I opened my eyes at once.

All around me were little ripples, for I was still being whirled around behind the *Hispaniola*. The schooner seemed to stagger in her course, and I saw her masts toss a little against the blackness of the night. Like the coracle, she was wheeling southward.

I glanced over my shoulder, and my heart jumped against my ribs. Right behind me was the glow of the campfire. The current had turned at right angles, sweeping both the tall schooner and the little dancing coracle around toward the open sea.

Then the schooner turned about twenty degrees. Shouting and footsteps onboard told me that the drunken combatants had recognized their disaster and postponed their quarrel.

I lay down flat in the bottom of that wretched boat and began to pray devoutly to my Maker. Surely the raging breakers at the exit of the anchorage would make an end of Jim Hawkins. I could not bear to watch my approaching fate.

Probably I lay that way for hours, beaten back and forth and often doused with flying spray, expecting the next plunge to be my last. I grew weary and numb. Sleep took me, and I dreamed of home and the old Admiral Benbow.

CHAPTER 24

THE CRUISE
OF THE CORACLE

Early the next morning I awoke to find myself a quarter mile southwest of Treasure Island. The visible land sloped steeply down from the Spyglass into tall seaside cliffs. The cliffs of Haulbowline Head were forty or fifty feet high, descending to a base of fallen rocks.

I thought I might paddle in and land near these cliffs, but I changed my mind when I saw the breakers and the monsters. The water beneath the cliffs was like a boiling kettle, with heavy sprays flying and flailing. Neither the coracle nor I could survive them.

As for the monsters, they were maybe forty or fifty huge, sluglike, slimy-looking things the size of cattle. Some crawled on flat rocks while others dove into the sea with great splashes. Their barking echoed off the cliff-sides. I have since learned that they were sea lions and entirely harmless. But at the time I far preferred to take my chances with the sea.

In the meantime I thought I had a better idea. North of Haulbowline Head, the land runs inward to a long stretch of sandy beach. Continuing north, it forms another peninsula. This pine-forested point is marked on the chart as Cape of the Woods. I remembered what Silver had said about the northward current running along the island's west coast. I felt I could make landfall at Cape of the Woods.

The wind kept blowing the same direction as the current, which was fortunate for me. Had it done otherwise the previous night, I doubt the coracle and I could have ridden out the conflict of wind and current. Today the coracle danced over the great, smooth swells like a little bird. I lay on my chest in the bottom, just looking over the edge, surprised how easily the crude little craft handled the sea.

After a little while I grew very bold. I sat up to try paddling, and learned right away that even a small shift in weight had drastic side effects. The boat ceased her gentle dancing and ran nose-first down a steep slope of water into the next wave. I was drenched and terrified. The moment I fell back into my old position, the coracle rode smoothly again. This had me quite concerned: if I could not safely steer her, how might I ever reach land?

I kept calm despite my fear. First I carefully bailed out the coracle with my sea-cap, careful not to shift my body too much. After that I lay peering over the edge again, studying the way my craft rode the waves.

The secret to her grace was her passenger's balance. If I did not unbalance her, the coracle avoided the steep, dangerous wave summits and found her own way to the lower, milder waves. I would have to lie still most of the time, but where the water was smooth I could paddle her a bit toward land. I lay on my elbows, awkward though the posture was, and every now and then gave a weak stroke to aim her ashore.

It was tedious, yet I visibly gained ground. I would miss the Cape of the Woods, but I had progressed some hundred yards east. I was close enough that I would surely make landfall at the next small peninsula of any sort—and I had better, for I was in a bad way.

My problem was thirst, torturous thirst. The heat of the sun and the drying saltwater on my lips made my throat burn and my brain ache. I remembered that a man might live for months without food but will die of thirst in a few days. The current did not care that I was sick with longing; it bore me past the trees into the next stretch of sea. What I saw there gave me a new idea.

Less than half a mile in front of me was the *Hispaniola*, her beautiful white sails partially set. It meant certain capture, but could the mutineers do worse to me than slow death by thirst? I was not sure whether to be glad or sorry. While trying to decide, I saw some extremely strange behavior from the *Hispaniola*.

When I first sighted the schooner, all her sails held wind. She was sailing about northwest, and I presumed the men onboard were circling the island on their way back to the anchorage. Presently she began to move more westward, and I thought they were after me. Then she fell directly against the wind. Her sails shivered.

I knew what that meant. The *Hispaniola* was 'taken aback' or 'in irons,' as sailors say. Any sailing ship in this condition is momentarily helpless. No competent seaman lets this happen, especially close to shore, for it can take precious minutes to recover. Ships are wrecked by just such errors.

"Clumsy fellows," said I. "They must still be drunk as owls." Had Captain Smollett been in command, I could imagine the severe tongue-lashing the guilty parties would have got.

Meanwhile the schooner gradually shifted course, caught wind, sailed swiftly for a minute or so, then came aback once more. I watched this happen several more times. Clearly nobody was steering. But where were the men? They must be dead drunk—if they were aboard at all, that is. Perhaps they had deserted her. If I could get on board, might I return the vessel to her captain?

The current bore both coracle and schooner southward at an equal rate, but the *Hispaniola*'s erratic sailing was my ally. Each time she hung in irons I gained upon her. If I got the opportunity to sit up and paddle, I could overhaul her. This seemed adventurous to me, and the prospect of a drink of water doubled my growing courage.

I got up and was welcomed almost instantly by another cloud of spray, but this time I stuck to my purpose. With all my strength and caution I paddled after the aimless *Hispaniola*. One time the sea hit me so hard I had to stop and bail, my heart fluttering like a bird. But gradually I learned to pilot the coracle without being swamped.

I was now gaining rapidly on the schooner, near enough to see that no one was on deck. Either the men were lying drunk below, or she was deserted. If they were drunk, I might batten down the hatches to trap them below deck, then do what I chose with the ship.

Then I saw my chance. The breeze fell very low for some seconds, and the current gradually turned the *Hispaniola* so that I was astern of her. The cabin window gaped open. The lamp was still burning. The mainsail drooped. She moved only with the current, and I was catching up.

I was not a hundred yards from her when the wind kicked up again. Her sails filled and took her away a bit, pitching clumsily. At first I despaired, but then things went my way. She came broadside to me, nearer every second. I could see the waves boiling white under her bow. She looked immensely tall compared to my lowly position.

I realized the danger almost too late to save myself. I was on the summit of one swell when the schooner lurched over the next, bringing me directly under the bow. I sprang to my feet and leaped without concern for my little craft. With one hand I caught a bow-rope, then hooked my foot over it.

As I clung there panting, a dull thump told me that the schooner had overrun the coracle. I was trapped on the *Hispaniola*.

CHAPTER 25

I STRIKE THE
JOLLY ROGER

I had just got up onto the bowsprit when the outermost jib-sail filled with an abrupt *crack*. The schooner trembled for a moment, nearly tossing me into the sea. I wasted no time crawling along the bowsprit to tumble headlong onto the *Hispaniola*'s deck near the forecastle.

There were many footprints here. Unsurprisingly, the mutineers had not spent much time swabbing decks. The mainsail blocked my sight of the afterdeck. The only moving object was a broken, empty bottle rolling about.

Suddenly the *Hispaniola* came about into the wind. The jibs behind me cracked aloud, the ship gave a sickening heave and shudder, and the mainsail's boom swung inboard. I could see the afterdeck.

There were the two watchmen, sure enough. Red-cap lay stiff on his back with his arms stretched out like a crucifix, his teeth bared in a horrid grin. Israel Hands was slumped against the ship's side, his face white as a candle. His hands lay open and empty.

For a while the ship bucked like a wild horse. The mainmast groaned as its boom swung randomly to and fro. Now and then a cloud of light spray burst over the side. It was strange indeed to see this great sophisticated ship having a worse time of it than my homemade, lopsided coracle.

The schooner's lurches shifted Red-cap's stiff body a little. They affected Hands more; with each sharp movement he slumped downward and astern. His face became hidden from me until I could see just an ear and some whiskers. Splashes of dark blood on deck around them suggested that they had killed each other in their drunken wrath.

While I was looking and wondering, the ship had a calm moment. Israel Hands turned partly around, gave a low, agonized moan, and forced himself back to a sitting position against the side. I pitied him until I remembered what I had overheard from the apple barrel.

I walked aft to the mainmast. "Come aboard, Mr. Hands," I said ironically.

He rolled his eyes around heavily, too far gone to express surprise. All he could do was to utter one word, "Brandy."

He might be near death. There was no time to lose. Dodging the sweep of the mainsail-boom across the deck, I went down into the cabin.

It was a pigpen. The mutineers had tracked in mud from the marsh. They had broken open every locked cabinet in search of the chart. The white bulkheads were covered with dirty handprints. Dozens of empty bottles clinked together in corners to the rolling of the ship. One of the doctor's medical books lay open on the table, with half the pages torn out, probably used to light pipes. In the midst of all this the lamp still cast a dim, smoky glow.

I went down into the cellar to discover all the barrels gone. An amazing number of the bottles had been drunk and thrown away. I was no great seaman, but I was surely a tavern-keeper's son. It was obvious that none of them could have spent a sober moment since the mutiny.

I searched about until I found a half-empty bottle of brandy for Hands. For myself I got some biscuits, pickled fruits, a great bunch of raisins, and a piece of cheese. I went on deck, put my food down out of Hands's reach, then went forward to the water keg. Only when I had drunk my fill of water did I give Hands the brandy.

He must have drunk a cupful before he set down the bottle. "Aye," said he, "by thunder, but I wanted some o' that!"

I had sat down already in my own corner and begun to eat. "Much hurt?" I asked him.

He grunted. "If that doctor was aboard," he said, "I'd be well enough soon, but I've no luck. As for that swab, he's good and dead," he added, indicating Red-cap. "He warn't no seaman anyhow. And where might you have come from?"

"Well," I said, "I've come aboard to take possession of this ship, Mr. Hands. You may consider me your captain until further notice."

He looked at me sourly but said nothing. Some of the color had come back into his cheeks, though he still looked sick and weak.

"By the way," I continued, "I am going to strike these miserable colors, Mr. Hands." I got up, dodged the boom again, and ran to the flag lines. Hand over hand I hauled down their cursed black flag and threw it overboard. "God save the king!" said I, waving my cap. "No more Captain Silver!"

Hands watched me keenly, his chin still on his breast, and at last he spoke. "I reckon, Cap'n Hawkins, you'll kind of want to get ashore now. S'pose we talks."

"Why, certainly, Mr. Hands," I said. "Speak up." I went back to my meal with a good appetite.

"This man," he began, nodding feebly at the corpse. "O'Brien were his name, an Irishman. He and me got the sails set, meaning to sail her back. Well, he's dead as bilge now. I don't see who's to sail the ship. Unless I gives you hints, you doesn't know how, far as I can tell. Now look here, Cap'n, if you gives me food and drink and a old scarf to tie my wound up, I'll tell you how to sail her. That's a fair offer, I says."

"I'll tell you one thing," I said. "I'm not going back to Captain Kidd's anchorage. I mean to get into North Inlet and beach her quietly there."

"Course you do," he cried. "Why, I ain't no lubber, and I ain't blind neither. I've lost and you've won. North Inlet? Why, I haven't no choice! I'd help you sail her up to Execution Dock in London town, by thunder!"

This seemed a sensible bargain to me, and I agreed. In three minutes I had the *Hispaniola* sailing easily before the wind along the coast of Treasure Island, with good hopes of turning the northern point before noon and reaching North Inlet before high tide. There we might beach her and land when the tide went out.

I lashed the steering tiller in place and went below to get my mother's soft silk handkerchief that she had given me. With it Hands and I bound up the great bleeding wound in his thigh. After he had eaten a little and had a little more brandy, he began to improve. He sat straighter, spoke louder and clearer, and looked on the road to recovery.

The breeze served us admirably. We skimmed past the high lands, then past low, sandy country with a few dwarf pine trees. Soon we had turned the corner of the rocky hill on the island's north end.

I was greatly elated with my new command. After all my fear and hard work, I now had bright, sunshiny weather, plenty of water and good things to eat. I had deserted my shipmates at the blockhouse, but I felt less guilty thanks to my great conquest.

My only concern was slumped against the side. The injured sailor's smile seemed like that of a haggard old man. But underneath there were glimmers of mocking treachery. The crafty, scornful eyes of Israel Hands were watching my every move.

CHAPTER 26

ISRAEL HANDS

The wind brought us easily around to the mouth of the North Inlet, and now we had a lot of time on our hands. With no anchor available, we had to wait for high tide to safely beach her. After many mistakes I got her sails set low enough that she might lie quiet, and we ate another meal in silence.

Hands kept that same uncomfortable smile. "Cap'n," he said at length, "s'pose you was to heave my old shipmate, O'Brien here, overboard. I ain't sayin' I'm to blame for his situation, now, but he don't make a good ornament, neither."

"I'm not strong enough, and I don't want to. There he stays," I said.

"This here's an unlucky ship, this *Hispaniola*, Jim," he went on, blinking. "Many poor seamen's been killed in this ship since you and me sailed from Bristol. Worst luck I ever seen. I'm no scholar;

you're a smart lad. Do you reckon a dead man is dead for good, or do he come alive again?"

"You can kill the body, Mr. Hands, but not the spirit, as you surely know," I replied. "O'Brien there is in another world, and may be watching us."

"Ah!" he said. "Well, that means killing someone is a waste of time. Howsoever, Jim, I never seen any spirits do much, so I'll take my chances with them. And now, I wonder if maybe...I'd be thankful if you'd go down and get me a bottle of that—ah, what's the word? Please bring me wine, Jim—this here brandy's too strong for my head."

Again the instincts of a tavern-boy served me well. For him to prefer wine was highly suspicious. And for such a drunkard to hesitate over any alcohol was even more so. The two together amounted to an alarm. I sensed that his whole request was a clumsy excuse to lure me below deck. What did he want to do?

Hands had no idea how transparent a liar he was. Perhaps he took me for a naive boy. His shifty eyes wandered about like any liar's. I answered promptly. It would be easy to conceal my suspicions from someone this stupid.

"Some wine?" I said. "Far better for you. Will you have white or red?"

"Well, I reckon it's about the blessed same to me, shipmate," he replied, "if it's strong and plenty of it."

"All right," I answered. "I'll see if I can't find you some, Mr. Hands. It may take some time."

I made as much noise as possible on the ladder. Once below I slipped off my shoes and ran quietly forward until I came to the forecastle ladder. I climbed up in silence to spy on the coxswain, and what I saw confirmed my worst suspicions.

The coxswain had risen to his hands and knees. Despite great pain he managed to drag himself quickly across the deck. In half a minute he was fishing something from a large coil of rope: a long, bloody knife. He tested the point, stashed the weapon in his jacket, and labored back to his slumping-place against the side.

So Hands meant to kill me. What then? Crawl across the island, perhaps, or fire the cannon to summon his comrades? In the meantime, though, we both needed the schooner beached in a safe, sheltered place from which she could be sailed away again. Surely he would not attack me until that was achieved.

While thinking about all this, I kept busy. I went back to the cabin, put on my shoes, and got a bottle of wine. I then reappeared on deck.

Hands looked up at me from his slumped position. I gave him the bottle, and he knocked its neck off with practiced skill. "Here's to luck!" he toasted, taking a good swig. He sat quiet for a while, then pulled out a stick of tobacco.

"Cut me a chew o' that, please, Cap'n

Hawkins, sir," he said, "for I haven't no knife nor enough strength if I had one. Ah, Jim, I reckon I'm done for! It'll likely be my last chew, lad, for I can tell I'm not long for this world."

"Well," I said, "I'll cut you some tobacco. But if I was in your situation, I would say my prayers like a Christian man."

"Why?" he said. "Now, you tell me why."

"Why?" I cried angrily, thinking of the bloody knife. "You have murdered and mutinied. You've lived in sin, lies, and blood. Your latest victim lies at your feet this moment, and you ask me why! For God's mercy, Mr. Hands, that's why."

Hands took a great drink of the wine and spoke solemnly.

"For thirty years," he said, "I've sailed the seas and seen good and bad, better and worse, fair weather and foul, thirst and hunger, knives and pistols and what not. Jim, I never seen any good come from being good. He who strikes first strikes best. Dead men don't bite. Them's my views. And now, look here," he added, suddenly changing his tone, "we've fooled about long enough. The tide's in. Just do as I say, Cap'n Hawkins, and we'll sail in and be done with it."

We had barely two miles to sail. They involved delicate navigation through the shallow, narrow entrance to the northern anchorage, but I was a prompt sailor and Hands was an excellent pilot. Our combined efforts brought her safely in.

North Inlet was a river-mouth, but it was longer and narrower than the southern anchorage. There were thick woods on both shores of the inlet. Ashore at the south end sat the decaying wreck of a three-masted ship. It had been there so long that bushes and flowers were growing on deck.

"Now," said Hands, "there's a fine spot to beach a ship. Fine flat sand, trees all around."

"And how will we get her to sea again?" I inquired.

"Why," he replied, "you put a rope around one of those big pines at low water, then fasten it to the capstan. At high water, all hands pull on the line, and she comes off sweet as can be. And now, boy, stand by to go about. We're near the spot now, and she's going too fast. Starboard a little—steady—starboard—larboard a little—steady—steady!" I obeyed, and soon the *Hispaniola* swung round and ran for the low shore.

I was so absorbed that I had quite forgot my peril and was craning my head over the starboard side. Had I not felt a sudden urge to turn around, I might have gone down without a fight. I turned to see Hands halfway toward me with the knife in his right hand.

We must both have cried out when our eyes met. Mine was terror; his was like the roar of a bull as he sprang.

Letting go the steering-tiller, I leapt aside toward the bow. The tiller sprang sharply away,

catching Hands across the chest and knocking him flat. While this had probably saved my life, there was no time to reflect; I hurried forward to the mainmast, where I halted and drew a pistol. He was on his feet and was coming for me.

I took a cool aim and pulled the trigger, but the hammer fell without flash or sound.

I cursed my neglect. Why had I not long since reloaded? The priming had got wet, of course.

Now I fled like a sheep before the butcher.

Hands was moving quickly despite his wound. His grizzled hair and furious face made him a terrible sight. My other pistol was probably in the same shape, and in any case I had no time to try it. If I let him corner me in the bow, I was dead. I put the thick mainmast between us and waited, every nerve tight.

First he paused. Then he made a series of false moves designed to lure me to the wrong side of the mast. I matched his every move, for I had played just such a game in my childhood among the rocks of Black Hill Cove—though never before with such a wildly beating heart. I could outmaneuver a wounded old seaman for some time, perhaps, but this could only end one way. I saw no hope of ultimate escape.

With that thought, the *Hispaniola* suddenly lurched, staggered, ground for an instant in the sand, then tilted far over to the port side. The deck lay at a sharp angle. About a barrelful of seawater splashed through the scupper-holes and pooled between the deck and the side.

The impact sent us both tumbling into the scuppers along with O'Brien's corpse. My head hit the coxswain's foot with a tooth-rattling crack, but I was the first back on my feet. Hands had got tangled up with the body.

The deck was too steeply tilted to run. I must find some new way of escape, and swiftly. The nearest mast was the mizzen, or rearmost. Quick as I could think, I leaped into the mizzenmast ropes, causing Hands's knife to miss me by no more than six inches. I climbed for my life.

When I was seated safely on the crosspiece, I halted for breath and looked down. Below me stood Israel Hands, his mouth hanging open in surprise and disappointment.

Now that I had a calm moment, I hastened to reload and reprime first one pistol, then the other, just to make sure. Hands saw me, hesitated, then put his knife in his teeth and hauled himself heavily into the ropes—a slow, painful process with his wounded leg.

He was scarcely a third of the way up when I finished my work. I took a pistol in each hand and called down to him. "One more step, Mr. Hands," I said, "and I'll blow your brains out! Dead men don't bite, you know," I added with a chuckle.

Hands stopped instantly. I could see his jaw working as he tried to think. He had no idea what to do, and I laughed aloud at his facial contortions. At last he took the dagger from his mouth and spoke.

"Jim," he said, "I reckon we're tangled, you and me, and we'll have to make terms. I'd have had you but for that there lurch, but I don't have no luck. I reckon I'll have to strike my colors. That's hard for me, a master mariner, to surrender to a ship's boy like you, Jim."

I listened with a smug smile. All of a sudden his right hand went back over his shoulder, and something sang like an arrow through the air. I felt a blow and then a sharp pain, and found myself pinned to the mast by the shoulder. In the horrid pain and surprise of the moment—I can hardly claim credit for doing it on purpose, nor for good aim—both my pistols went off and fell out of my hands.

They did not fall alone. The coxswain gave a choked cry, let go the ropes and plunged headfirst into the water.

CHAPTER 27

"PIECES OF EIGHT"

The *Hispaniola* was leaning so sharply that her masts hung far out over the water. Hands had been just far enough up the mast to miss the ship's side. He rose once to the surface in a lather of foam and blood, then sank again for good. As the water settled, I could see him lying huddled up on the clean, bright sand of the shallow bottom. After a time I knew he was dead, both shot and drowned.

In my excitement I had taken little note of my own condition, but now a wave of terror and fainting coursed through me. The knife held my shoulder to the mast by my skin and coat. Blood ran down my back and chest, but not much. I had a terrible fear of falling into the water alongside Hands's corpse. I shut my eyes as if to hide the peril and clung with both hands until my nails ached.

It took me some moments to pull myself together. I must remove the knife, I thought, and reached for it. As I did, my frayed nerves gave way, my body shuddered as though I were suddenly freezing, and the difficulty was solved. The blade tore through the pinch of skin and coat, liberating me.

I was now bleeding more, to be sure, but not dangerously. I climbed down to the deck by the starboard-side ropes, then went below to bind up my wound. I could still use my arm without too much pain. I went back on deck, the sole master of the schooner.

Hands had got one thing right: O'Brien's body was not an attractive sight. He still lay tumbled against the side, like some horrible discarded puppet.

Once I would have hesitated, but my adventures had made me less squeamish. I took him by the waist like a sack of grain and gave him a good heave. He went overboard with a noisy plunge; the red cap came off and floated on the surface. As soon as the splash subsided, I could see him lying across his murderer's knees. I was surprised to see that, despite his youth, O'Brien had been bald.

I was now alone on the ship. The tide had just turned. Sunset approached. The evening breeze had come up. In spite of the shelter of the anchorage, the sails began to rattle and flap in the wind. If I did not act quickly, the ship might be blown off her sandy perch. Once she was adrift, I would be unable to handle her.

I easily lowered the jib-sails on the bow, but the huge mainsail was another matter. Its boom had swung over so far that the aft lower tip of the sail dipped into the water. My only remedy was to cut the sail loose. By climbing I could reach every rope but the one under the water, and before long the ship's primary sail trailed out across the water. I could do no more for the *Hispaniola*. Like me, she now depended upon luck. I needed to rejoin my comrades.

By this time the whole anchorage had fallen into shadow. The schooner settled over a bit more to port. I scrambled forward and looked over the side. The water looked shallow enough. I took hold of the anchor rope, the same one I had cut sitting in the coracle. It was an easy matter to lower myself into the waist-deep water and wade ashore.

Before setting forth I looked with some pride upon my achievement. I had cleared the schooner of mutineers and got her ready for our side to recapture and sail. The damage I had done could be easily repaired. I was eager to boast of my feat to my comrades. I might be blamed a bit for deserting, but the recapture of the *Hispaniola* was a fine answer to any fault on my part. Even Captain Smollett would have to praise me for handing him back his command.

In the near-darkness I set out toward the block-house and my companions. If memory served, I would have to cross a stream. I decided that it would be better to do so inland where the stream would be smaller. The woods were not dense, and I made good time around the corner of the hill.

While wading the stream, I remembered that I was near the spot of my encounter with Ben Gunn. I made sure to stay alert. In the dusk I saw a wavering glow, most likely that of Ben's cooking fire. Why did he show himself so carelessly? Wasn't he afraid Silver would spot it? Something did not make sense.

As the night fell blacker it became harder to navigate. I kept tripping over bushes and stumbling into sandy hollows. After a time I saw a broad silvery moon low down through the trees. When the moon fully rose I made much swifter progress.

When I neared the stockade, I controlled my impatience and moved more warily. It would have been a poor end of my adventures to be shot down mistakenly by my own party. The moon was casting more light, but in front of me a different sort of glow showed through the trees. It was red and hot and flickering. I could not imagine what it might be.

At last I reached the edge of the clearing. Most of it still lay in shadow, with long silvery streaks of moonlight peering through. On the

other side of the house an immense fire had
burned itself into glowing red embers. There was
not a soul stirring, nor any sound but the breeze.

I stopped in wonder and fear. At the captain's
orders, we had conserved our firewood. Building
any sort of bonfire would have been unthinkable.
I began to suspect something very wrong, and
started to slink around the eastern, darkest side of
the blockhouse clearing. When I thought I was
quite well-hidden, I climbed over the stockade.

For safety's sake, I crawled the last distance to
the porch. I heard a heart-warming sound: my
friends snoring peacefully in their sleep. At another time it would have irritated me. But now it was
the sweetest music in the world. It also meant that
they kept a very poor watch. A good thing, I
thought, that I was not Silver and his lads creeping
up on them. This came of having the captain
wounded. I was partly at fault for my absence had
cost them one of their few able-bodied watchmen.

When I was inside the porch, I stood up in the
doorway. It was too dark inside to see anything.
There were only two sounds: the steady drone of
snoring, and a small occasional sort of flicking or
pecking noise. I walked inside with my arms out to
avoid running into anything. I had an amusing
thought: I would lie down in my own place as
though nothing were amiss. When they found me
the next morning, I would have a good laugh.

My foot struck a sleeper's leg. He turned and

groaned, but did not awaken.

Suddenly a shrill voice pierced the darkness: "Pieces of eight! Pieces of eight! Pieces of eight!" and so forth, like a deranged cuckoo clock.

Silver's green parrot, Captain Flint! She had made the pecking noise. She kept better watch than any human being, and had now publicly announced my arrival.

I had no time to recover. The sleepers awoke and sprang up. I heard Silver give a mighty curse, then cry out, "Who goes?"

I turned to run, struck violently against some-one, bounced off, and ran right into someone else's arms. I was caught.

"Bring a torch, Dick," Silver said when the ruckus died down.

One of the men left the log-house and soon returned with a burning torch.

TREASURE ISLAND

PART 6

CAPTAIN SILVER

CHAPTER 28

IN THE
ENEMY'S CAMP

The red torchlight proved my worst fears true. It was bad enough that the pirates had captured the house with its food and cognac supplies. The absence of any prisoners was ten times worse. My heart sank, for I could only assume they were all dead. I wished I had perished with them.

Only six mutineers were left alive. Five of them rose shakily to their feet; it was clear they had been sleeping off a drunk. The sixth did not stand, but propped on an elbow; his pale cheeks and the bloody bandage on his head said why.

The parrot sat on Long John's shoulder, grooming her feathers. He looked paler and sterner than before. His once-fine clothing was now muddy and torn.

"So," he said, "here's Jim Hawkins, shiver my timbers! Well, lad, glad to see you."

He sat down across the brandy cask. While he spoke, he filled and lit a pipe.

"Gentlemen, wake up! You needn't stand up for Mr. Hawkins. He'll excuse you, of course. Jim, you're a pleasant surprise for poor old John. I seen you were smart when first I met you, but this here I don't understand one bit, I don't."

I did not answer, of course, but merely stood with my back against the wall. I looked Silver in the face with what I hoped was defiance. My heart was filled with despair.

Silver calmly took a whiff or two of his pipe, then went on.

"Now, you see, Jim, being as you *are* here, I'll tell you my thinking. I've always liked you, I have. You reminds me of myself when I was young and handsome. I always wanted you to have your share and be rich. Now, son, it's your only choice. Cap'n Smollett's a fine seaman, but stiff on discipline, and he's against you. The doctor has gone against you—'ungrateful scamp' was his words. You can't go back to your own crew, for they won't have you. Either you start a third ship's company all by your lonesome, or you'll have to join with Cap'n Silver."

So my friends were still alive. I partly believed Silver's statement—the cabin party might well be angry at me for leaving—but I was more relieved than distressed.

"I won't threaten you, though here you are," continued Silver. "I'm all for talking things through. I never seen good come out o' threatening. If you like the service, well, you'll join as my shipmate. And if you don't, Jim, why, you're free to answer no. No seaman alive'd give you fairer terms, lad, you can be sure!"

"Must I answer right now?" I asked in a shaky voice. Through all this sneering talk, I could feel the threat of death hanging over me. My cheeks burned and my heart beat painfully.

"Lad," said Silver, "no one's a-pressing you. Take your bearings. We won't hurry you, mate. We likes your company so much, you see."

"Well," I said, growing a bit bolder, "if I'm to choose, I have a right to know what's happened to my friends."

Silver spoke in the same gracious tone: "Yesterday morning, Mr. Hawkins, down came Doctor Livesey with a flag of truce. Says he, 'Cap'n Silver, you're sold out. Ship's gone.' We had taken drink, I admit. We wasn't keeping an eye on the ship. When we looked, by thunder, the old ship was gone! 'Well,' says the doctor, 'let's bargain.' We bargained, him and I, and here we are: stores, brandy, blockhouse, the firewood you was thoughtful enough to cut, the whole kit. As for them, they've tramped off, to wheres I don't know."

He took another draw at his pipe.

"As for you, Jim," he went on, "here's the last word that was said: 'How many are you?' says I.

'Four,' says he; 'and one of us wounded. As for that boy, I don't know where he is, confound him,' says he, 'nor I don't much care. We're about sick of him.' These was his words."

"Is that all?" I asked.

"Well, it's all that you're to hear, my son," returned Silver.

"And now I am to choose?"

"You must," said Silver.

"Well," said I, "I can see what will happen to me, and I do not much care. I've seen too many die since I fell in with you. But I have a thing or two to tell *you*," I said. I grew excited as I continued.

"The first is this: all your plans are in shambles—ship lost, treasure lost, men lost, your whole business wrecked—and *I* did it! I was in the apple barrel, and I heard you, John, and you, Dick Johnson, and Hands, who is now at the bottom of the sea. Before the hour was out I repeated your every word. I cut the schooner loose, and killed your men aboard her, and brought her where you'll never see her again. I have the last laugh, and I do not fear you. Kill me or spare me. I don't care. But I'll say one thing: if you spare me, bygones are bygones, and when you fellows are in court for piracy, I'll help you if I can. Now *you* choose. Kill another and do yourselves no good, or spare me and keep a witness to save you from the gallows."

I was out of breath. To my wonder, not a man moved, but all sat staring at me like sheep. "And now, Mr. Silver," I said, "I believe you're the best man here. If worse comes to worst, I'll thank you to tell the doctor I died like a man."

"I'll bear it in mind," said Silver in a very strange tone. I could not decide whether he was impressed with my courage or amused by my request.

"I've a point to make," cried the old tanned seaman—Morgan by name—whom I had seen in Long John's pub along the Bristol docks. He pointed at me. "It was him that knowed Black Dog."

"See here, Tom," growled the sea cook. "I've point of my own to make, by thunder! It was this same boy that swiped the chart from Billy Bones. Every time, we've run hard aground on a rock named Jim Hawkins!"

"Then I'll settle it here!" said Morgan with an oath. He sprang up, drawing his knife.

"Hold, there!" cried Silver. "Tom Morgan, you think you're cap'n here, perhaps? Cross me, and you'll go where many a good man's gone before you—some hung, and some overboard, all to feed the fishes. Never a man looked me between the eyes and seen a good day afterwards, Tom Morgan. Think about that."

Morgan paused, but a hoarse murmur rose from the others.

"Tom's right," said one.

"I got mistreated by one captain long

enough," added another. "I'll be hanged if I'll be hazed by you, John Silver."

"Did any of you gentlemen want to have it out with *me*?" roared Silver, bending far forward, his pipe still glowing in his right hand. "Him that wants a fight shall get it. You know the way. You're all gentlemen o' fortune. Let him that dares take a cutlass, and before that pipe's empty I'll see the color of his insides, never mind my crutch!"

Not a man stirred. Not a man answered.

"See?" he added, returning his pipe to his mouth. "Well, you're a fine lot. I'm cap'n here by election. I'm elected because I'm the best man by a long sea mile. Since you won't fight, as gentlemen o' fortune should, then by thunder you'll obey! I like that boy, now. He's more a man than any of you in this here house. Let me see who dares lay a hand on him."

There was a long pause. I stood straight up against the wall, my heart still going like a sledgehammer, but with a ray of hope. Silver leaned back against the wall, calm but keeping a close eye on his unruly followers. They drew gradually together at the far end of the blockhouse, whispering in low tones. One after another they looked up nervously at Silver.

"You has a lot to say," remarked Silver, spitting far into the air. "Let me hear it, or be silent."

"Asking your pardon, sir," returned an ill-looking man in his thirties, "maybe you'll remember the rules. This crew don't like being bullied, and they've rights just like other crews. You said you value talking things over; we're talking things over. I ask your pardon, sir, acknowledging you as captain at this moment; but I claims my right to step outside for a council." With an elaborate seasalute, the sick man stepped coolly outside. The rest followed his example, each saluting and explaining as he passed. "According to rules," said one. "Forecastle council," said Morgan. The man with the head wound was last out, leaving Silver and me alone with the torch.

The sea cook instantly removed his pipe.

"Now, look you here, Jim Hawkins," he said in a low, steady whisper, "you're within half a plank of death, or worse, torture. They're going to throw me out, but John'll stand by you through thick and thin. I didn't plan to. I admit it. I was angered about losing that money, and being hanged as well. But when you spoke up manly-like, Jim, I says to myself, 'You stand by Hawkins, John, and Hawkins'll stand by you. You're his last card, and by thunder, John, he's yours!' Back to back, says I. You save Jim, and he'll save your neck!"

I began to understand. "You mean all's lost?" I asked.

"Aye, by gum!" he answered. "Once I looked into that bay, Jim Hawkins, and seen no schooner—I knew it was up. As for that council outside, they're outright fools and cowards. I'll save your life from them if I can, Jim, and fair's fair: you save Long John from swinging."

I was bewildered. His hope seemed ridiculous. The ringleader in a piracy or mutiny was always hanged.

"I'll do what I can," I said.

"It's a bargain!" cried Long John. "You speak up for me, and by thunder, I've a chance!"

He hobbled to the torch and relit his pipe. "Understand me, Jim," he said, returning. "I'm no fool. I'm on squire's side now. I know you've got that ship safe somewheres. How you done it, I don't know. I guess Hands and O'Brien turned soft—I never much trusted either man. Listen, Jim: I know when the game's up. Ah, a brave young lad like you—we might have done great things together!"

He got himself a drink of cognac.

"Will you have some, messmate?" he asked. I refused. "Well, I'll take a cup myself, Jim," he said. "I need it, for there's trouble on hand. Speaking o' trouble, why did that doctor give me the chart, Jim?"

My face expressed such obvious wonder he saw it was useless to ask more.

"Ah, well, he did," said he. "And no doubt there's a reason—though bad or good, I can't tell."

He took another swallow of the brandy, shaking his head like a man expecting the worst.

CHAPTER 29

The Black Spot Again

The pirates spent a long time in council. Partway through it, one returned to the block-house. He tossed Silver an insincere salute and said, "Cap'n Silver, we'd take kindly to the loan of that torch."

"You may," said Long John calmly. After the man had left us in darkness, Silver added to me in a friendly tone, "There's a breeze coming, Jim."

I turned to look out the nearest firing-port. The conspirators were huddled together about the torchlight halfway down the slope. One knelt in their midst with an open knife and a book in his hands. As I wondered what he was up to, the kneeling figure stood up. The whole party moved toward the house.

"Here they come," said I, moving away from the firing-port so as not to be caught snooping.

"Well, let 'em come, lad," said Silver cheerily. "I've still a shot in my locker."

The door opened, and five of them pushed one man forward slowly. He held his right hand closed in front of him.

"Step up, lad," cried Silver. "I won't harm you. I know the rules."

The pirate passed something to Silver, then slipped quickly back to his companions. The sea cook looked at the piece of paper in his hand.

"The black spot! I thought so," he observed. "Why, you've gone and cut this out of a Bible. Cutting a Bible is the worst of luck! What fool's done this?"

"Ah, there!" said Morgan. "I told you no good'd come of that!"

"Well, you'll all hang now, I reckon," continued Silver. "What soft-headed lubber had a Bible?"

"It was Dick," said one.

"Then Dick best get to prayers," Silver said. "Dick's luck is over, and you can be sure of that."

The tall, sickly man spoke up.

"Hold that talk, John Silver," he said. "This crew has tipped you the black spot in full council, as the rules allow. It's your duty to turn it over and read, then you can talk."

"Thanky, George Merry," replied the sea cook. "You always was businesslike, and knows the rules by heart, I'm pleased to see. Well, what is it?" Silver glanced at the paper. "Ah! 'Deposed,' is it? You wrote very pretty, George—maybe you'll be cap'n next? Just loan me that torch again, will you? My pipe's gone low."

"Come, now," said George, "you don't fool us no more. You're a funny man, but you're tipped, and now maybe you'll help vote a new cap'n."

"I thought you knowed the rules," returned Silver contemptuously. "Leastways, I do. I'm still your cap'n, till you says your grievances and I reply. After that, we'll see who's with you."

"Oh," replied George, "don't fool yourself, John Silver. We six are all together. First, you've made a hash of this cruise—you can't argue other-wise. Second, you let the enemy out o' this here trap for nothing. Third, you wouldn't let us go after them. We see through you, John Silver; you want to play both sides. And then, fourth, there's this here boy."

"Is that all?" asked Silver quietly.

"Enough, too," retorted George. "We'll all hang and dry in the sun for your bungling."

"Well now, look here, I'll answer these four points," rejoined Silver. "A hash o' this cruise? You all know what *I* wanted. If you'd listened, we'd all be healthy aboard the *Hispaniola* tonight with full stomachs and a hold full of treasure, by thunder! But who forced my hand? Why, it was Anderson, and Hands, and you, George Merry! You're the last of the meddlers alive. And you dare try to be cap'n over me—after you sank the lot of us! This beats any yarn I ever heard!"

Silver paused. I could see his words hit home on more than one face.

"That's for point number one," cried Silver in outrage. "Why, I wonder why your mothers ever let you come to sea. Gentlemen o' fortune! I reckon tailors is your trade."

"Go on, John," said Morgan. "Answer the others."

"Ah, the others!" returned John. "You say this cruise is bungled—by gum, you've no idea how bad it's bungled! We're so near the gallows it makes my neck stiff. You've seen 'em hanged in chains, pecked by birds, seamen pointing 'em out as they pass. 'Who's that?' says one. 'Why, that's John Silver. I knowed him well,' says another. That's about where we are, thanks to Merry, and Hands, and Anderson, and other fools of you. As for number four—that boy? Shiver my timbers—a hostage might be our last chance. Kill him? Not me, mates! And number three? You don't like having a real college doctor to tend you? John, how's your broken head feeling? George Merry, wasn't you shaking with the fever not six hours ago? You're sicker'n a landsman on his first cruise, you are!"

Silver waited a moment, then went on. "And maybe you didn't know the *Hispaniola*'s sister ship was coming along soon? When she does, we'll see who'll be glad to have a hostage. And as for

point number two, and why I made a bargain—
well, you came crawling to me to make it—and
you'd have starved if I hadn't. But that's nothing.
Look there!" He threw a paper on the floor.

It was the chart from Billy Bones's sea chest,
with the three red crosses on yellow paper. Why
the doctor had given Silver the precious docu-
ment, I had no idea.

The surviving mutineers were ecstatic. They
leaped upon it like cats on a mouse with a storm of
oaths and cackles and cries. They tore it from each
other's hands as though it were the very gold they
had come for.

"Yes," said one, "that's Flint, sure enough.
His initials, and his sign of the clove-hitch knot,
like he always done."

"But how do we get away with it, now that
Cap'n Silver's misplaced his ship?" asked George.

Silver sprang up and growled, "One more
word out of you, George, and I'll call you down
and fight you. How do we get the treasure home,
you ask? You ought to figure that out yourself,
curse you, since you and the rest interfered and
lost me my schooner! But you can't. You ain't got
the brains of a cockroach, George Merry, but you
can at least speak civil—and you will. Take my
word on that."

"That's fair enough," said old Morgan.

"Fair! I reckon so," said the sea cook. "You
lost the ship; I found the way to the treasure.

Who's the better man? And now I resign, by thunder! Elect whom you please to be your cap'n now; I'm done with it."

"Silver!" they cried. "Barbecue forever! Barbecue for cap'n!"

"So that's the tune, is it?" cried the sea cook. "George, I reckon you'll have to wait, friend. And be glad I was never a revengeful man. And now, shipmates, this black spot? All it means now is that Dick's spoiled his Bible and his luck, and no more."

"It'll do to swear on, won't it?" growled Dick, a little uneasily.

"A Bible with a bit cut out!" scoffed Silver. "A promise on it ain't no more binding than one on a song-book." He tossed me the page. "Here, Jim—here's a curiosity for you," said Silver.

It was the very last page of the Bible. One side was blank. The other contained the last few verses of the Book of Revelation, and these words struck sharply into my mind: "Outside are the dogs and murderers." A black spot had been marked in wood ash on the printed side. On the blank side was written, also in ash: "Depposed." I have that paper beside me as I write, but no trace of writing now remains.

The night's business was over. Soon after, with a drink all round, we lay down to sleep. Silver's only revenge on George was to put him on watch, on pain of death should he prove unfaithful.

For a long time my mind was too active to sleep. I thought of my danger, the man I had slain that afternoon, and above all Silver's remarkable game. With one hand he kept the mutineers together; with the other he grasped at any means to save his miserable life. He snored peacefully, yet despite his wickedness I felt badly for him. He was almost sure to hang.

CHAPTER 30

THE WORD OF HONOR

At daybreak we were all awakened by a clear, hearty voice from the woods: "Block-house, ahoy! Here's the doctor."

I was glad to hear Dr. Livesey's voice, but also ashamed. My unpredictable behavior had brought me here among the criminals. How could I look him in the eyes? I ran to look out a firing-hole, and saw him standing knee-deep in the low fog, just as Silver had once done.

"Doctor! Good morning to you, sir!" cried Silver good-naturedly. "Bright and early, to be sure. Your patients is all doing well and merry. George, shake up your timbers, son, and help Dr. Livesey aboard." He sounded just as if he were back home supervising his tavern. "We've quite a surprise for you too, sir—a new boarder, and looking fit after a good sleep."

Dr. Livesey had got across the stockade and was near the porch. I could hear the change in his voice as he said, "Not Jim?"

"The very same Jim as ever," Silver said.

The doctor stopped. After a few speechless seconds, he continued inside. "Well, well," he said at last, "duty first and pleasure afterward, as you might have said yourself, Silver. Let's see these patients."

He gave me only a grim nod before tending to the sick. Though he surely must have known he was in great danger, he spoke to his patients as if this were an ordinary professional visit in a quiet English home. The effect on the men was amazing. They acted like he was still ship's doctor, and they still faithful seamen.

"You're doing well, my friend," he said to the fellow with the bandaged head, "but you had a close shave. Your head must be hard as iron. Well, George, how goes it? You're a pretty color; your liver is upside down. Did you take that medicine? Did he take it, men?"

"Aye, aye, sir, he took it, sure enough," returned Morgan.

"Good. After all, I am mutineers' doctor—or prison doctor, as I prefer to say," said Dr. Livesey pleasantly. "It's my duty not to lose a man for King George—God bless him!—and the gallows."

The rogues looked uncomfortably at each other but said nothing. Then one said, "Dick don't feel well, sir."

"Doesn't he?" replied the doctor. "Well, step up here, Dick, and let me see your tongue. No wonder! You have a serious fever, my man."

"Ah, there," said Morgan, "that came of spoiling Bibles."

"That came—as you put it—of being such great fools you camped in a disease-ridden swamp," retorted the doctor. "Likely you will all suffer from malaria. Silver, I'm surprised at you. You're less of a fool than many, but you have no idea of the rules of good health."

They took their medicines and criticism with comical humility. "Well," he added, "that's done for today. And now I wish to talk with that boy, please." He nodded toward me.

George Merry was at the door, spluttering over some bad-tasting medicine. He swung round toward the doctor, swore, and cried, "No!"

Silver struck the barrel with his open hand. "Silence!" he roared and looked angrily around.

"Doctor," he went on in his usual tones, "I was a-thinking of that, knowing how fond you was of the boy. We're all humbly grateful for your kindness, and trusts you so much that we takes our medicines down like rum. Hawkins, you're poor born, but you're a young gentleman. Will you give me your gentlemanly word of honor not to slip your anchor cable?"

"I give you my word that I will not try to escape," I pledged.

"Then, Doctor," said Silver with a few dark looks at the men, "just climb outside o' that stockade, and I'll bring the boy to the wall, and you may speak together as long as you wish. Good day to you, sir, and compliments to the squire and Cap'n Smollett."

The men's disapproval now exploded like a bombshell. Everyone rightly accused Silver of trying to make a separate peace for himself, at their expense. It was so obvious I could not imagine how he could calm them. But he was twice the man they were, and his victory the night before gave him prestige. Calling them all kinds of fools, he bellowed, "Can't you see that of course Jim needs to speak to the doctor?" He waved the chart in their faces. "Break the treaty, on the very day we're a-hunting the treasure? No, by thunder! Till the time comes, I'll keep that doctor happy, no matter what it takes. Now, all hands to light the fire and start the breakfast." He stalked out with his hand on my shoulder, leaving them silenced but unconvinced.

"Slow, lad, slow," he said. "If they see us hurry, they might turn on us." We slowly advanced across the sand to where the doctor awaited us outside the stockade. As soon as we were within easy speaking distance Silver stopped.

"You'll note this, Doctor," he said. "The boy'll tell you how I saved his life, though it turned the men against me. You know my situation. I'm gambling with the last breath in my body. And now the boy's life hangs in the balance as well. Won't you give me a bit of hope, for the sake of both Jim an' me?"

Silver was a changed man. His cheeks seemed to have fallen in, and his voice trembled.

"Why, John, you're not afraid?" asked Dr. Livesey.

"I'm no coward, not I!" Silver snapped his fingers. "If I was afeard, I wouldn't admit it. But I'll admit, the gallows give me the shakes. I never seen a better man than you, Doctor, and you'll remember what good I done along with the bad. Now, see, I step aside and leave you and Jim alone in good faith. I couldn't do more, could I?"

Silver stepped back out of earshot, sat down on a tree-stump, and began to whistle. He kept a close eye on me, the doctor, and on his unruly crew as they made the breakfast-fire.

"So, Jim," said the doctor sadly, "here you are. You have brewed bitter tea, my boy, and now you must drink it. Heaven knows I cannot blame you, but I will say this: you would not have dared leave when the Captain was well. It was downright cowardly of you to desert when he was too ill to object, by George!"

I admit that I began to cry. "Doctor," I said, "you might forgive me. I have blamed myself enough, and will lose my life anyway. Without Silver's protection I would already be dead. Death

I can face. I deserve it. But if they start to torture me—"

"Jim," the doctor interrupted in a very different voice, "I can't have that. Come over, and we'll run for it."

"Doctor," said I, "I gave my word."

"I know, I know," he cried. "That can't be helped. I'll take the blame, Jim, but I cannot let you stay. One jump, and we'll run for it like antelopes."

"No," I replied. "You wouldn't break your own word, nor would the squire or captain; nor will I. Silver trusted me; I gave my word, and back I go. But, Doctor, please let me finish. Under torture, I might tell them where the ship is. I got her, by luck and daring, and she lies in North Inlet on the southern beach, just below high water. At half tide she must be high and dry."

"The ship!" exclaimed the doctor. I quickly told him my adventures. He listened in silence. When I finished, he spoke again.

"There is an odd fate in this. Every step, it's you that saves our lives. How can we let you lose yours? You found out the plot; you found Ben Gunn—the best deed you will ever do if you live to be ninety. Now wait a moment."

Dr. Livesey called Silver over to us; he came near. "Silver! A piece of advice for you: don't be in any great hurry after that treasure."

"Why, sir, I has to," said Silver. "Asking your

pardon, sir, if I don't look for it, both me and the boy are lost for certain, take my word for that."

"Well, then," replied the doctor, "I'll tell you this: when you find it, look out for storms."

"Sir," said Silver, "man to man, now you've said too much and too little. I can't know why you left the blockhouse, nor why you gave me that there chart, can I? Yet I done like you asked, without a word of mercy from you. But this here's too much. If you won't tell me plain what you mean, just say so and I'll leave."

"No," said the doctor, "I've no right. It's not my secret to tell. If it were, I give you my word I would tell you. But I've gone as far as I dare, and I'll give you a bit of hope as well: if we both get out of this wolf-trap alive, I'll do my best to save you, short of perjury."

Silver beamed. "You couldn't say fairer, sir, not if you was my mother," he cried.

"Well, that's my first concession," added the doctor. "My second is a piece of advice. Keep Jim close beside you, and when you're in trouble, call out. I'm off to try and get you help. Good-bye, Jim."

Dr. Livesey shook hands with me through the stockade, nodded to Silver, and went briskly off into the woods.

CHAPTER 31

THE TREASURE HUNT— FLINT'S POINTER

"Jim," said Silver when we were alone, "now I've saved your life, and you've saved mine; and I'll not forget it. I seen the doctor waving you to run for it, and I seen you say no, as plain as hearing. Now I've got hope again, thanks to you. And now we're in for a bad surprise on this treasure hunting, and I don't like it. You and me must stick close, and we'll save our necks in spite o' fate and fortune."

Just then a man called out that breakfast was ready, and we soon sat down to our biscuit and bacon. They had lit an enormous fire, and cooked three times what we could eat. After breakfast, one of them threw the leftovers into the fire and laughed as it blazed and roared. I had never before seen men so wasteful, so careless of tomorrow.

Silver ate with Captain Flint upon his shoulder.

Rather than criticize their recklessness, he spoke with his greatest cunning yet.

"Aye, mates," said he, "it's lucky you have Barbecue to think for you. I got what I wanted, I did. Sure enough, they have the ship; where, I don't know, but once we hit the treasure, we'll have to find out. And then, mates, us that has the boats has the upper hand."

His words seemed to restore their confidence, and perhaps his own as well.

"As for our hostage," he continued, "that's his last talk, I guess, with his dear friends. I've got my news, and thanky to him for that; but it's done. I'll tie a line on him when we go treasure hunting, just in case of accidents. Once we get the ship and treasure both out to sea, why, we'll surely give Mr. Hawkins his share."

The men were in a good humor now, but I wasn't. Silver was a double traitor. If this scheme looked promising, he would carry it through. He was still playing both camps, and he would surely prefer wealth and freedom to a narrow escape from hanging, which was the best he could expect on our side. And even if events forced him to keep his bargain with Dr. Livesey, what danger lay before us! When Silver was found out—and he would be—how could a cripple and a boy fight for their lives against five hearty seamen?

I also worried over my friends' behavior. Why desert the stockade and hand Silver the chart?

What had the doctor meant by warning Silver to "look out for storms"? I had no appetite. My heart was heavy as I departed behind my captors on the treasure hunt.

We would have made a curious sight, all in soiled sailor clothes and all but me armed to the teeth. Silver had two muskets, a great cutlass, and a pistol in each pocket. Captain Flint perched on his shoulder, babbling sea-talk. One end of a rope was tied about my waist, and the other end Silver held in his powerful hand. I was led like a dancing bear.

The other men were loaded down with picks, shovels, pork, bread, and brandy. All our food and drink came from the bartered supplies. Silver had been right the night before. If he had not bargained with the doctor, his mutineers would have had to drink clear water and hunt their food. They would have resented not having rum, and few sailors are good shots. Likely they would also be short of powder, and would tend to waste what they had.

We went down to where the two boats were beached. Even these showed evidence of the pirates' drunken foolhardiness. One had a broken crosspiece, and both held muddy water. We divided ourselves between the two boats and launched them into the anchorage.

As we rowed, the men debated over the chart. The red cross was far too large to be precise, and the note on the back was cryptic. As you may remember, it said:

> **Tall tree, Spyglass shoulder, bearing a point to the N. of N.N.E.**
> **Skeleton Island E.S.E. and by E.**
> **Ten feet.**

We clearly had to begin by locating a tall tree. The "Spyglass shoulder" was most likely the wooded plateau ahead of us, two or three hundred feet high, joining the Spyglass on the north. Among the pines atop the plateau grew a few other, taller types of trees. It was by no means obvious which was the "tall tree" Captain Flint meant, but every man had a strong opinion as to which it was. Long John could only shrug his shoulders and tell them to wait until we arrived.

Silver ordered us to row easily and conserve our energy, so it took us quite a long time. We eventually landed at the mouth of the stream running down a woody valley of the Spyglass. The soft, mushy ground slowed our climb at first. As the hill grew steeper, the ground grew dry and rocky. Here and there were spicy nutmeg trees and fragrant, flowery shrubs. The air was fresh and clean. It was the nicest place I had yet seen on Treasure Island.

The party fanned out, shouting and leaping here and there. In the center followed Silver with me in tow. It was heavy going for him, especially on loose rock or gravel. I had to help him from time to time so he wouldn't stumble backward down the hill.

When we were near the plateau's edge, the

man farthest to the left gave a cry of alarm. The others ran in his direction.

"He can't 'a found the treasure," said old Morgan, hurrying past us from the right, "for that's up on top."

He had found something else. At the foot of a large pine lay a human skeleton wearing a few shreds of clothing. The skull still held a few wisps of hair. The vines growing through the remains had disarranged some of the bones. I believe every one of us felt a chill in his heart.

"He was a seaman," said George Merry, who had been bold enough to go close and examine the rags. "Leastways, this is good sea-cloth."

"Aye, aye," said Silver; "you wouldn't reckon to find a bishop here. But what sort of a way is that for bones to lie? 'Tain't natural."

Indeed it wasn't. Except where either birds or the vines had disturbed his posture, the man's bones lay perfectly straight. His feet pointed straight down, and his arms and hands were aimed directly above his head as though he were diving.

"I've taken a notion into my old numbskull," observed Silver. "Take the compass. There's the tip-top o' Skeleton Island, stickin' out like a tooth. Just take a bearing, will you, along the line of them bones."

It was done. The body pointed straight in the direction of the island, and the compass read E.S.E. by E.

"I thought so," cried the cook. "This here is a pointer to the loot. But, by thunder, it makes me cold to think of Flint. This is one of his jokes, no mistake. Him and these six was alone here; he killed 'em all, and laid this one down here by compass, shiver my timbers! They're long bones, and the hair's yellow; that would be Allardyce. Remember Allardyce, Tom Morgan?"

"Aye," returned Morgan; "He owed me money, and took my knife ashore with him."

"We might find it lying around," said another. "Flint warn't the kind to pick a seaman's pocket; and the birds would leave it be."

"By the powers, that's true!" cried Silver.

"There ain't a penny nor a buckle left here. Not a thing," said Merry, still feeling among the bones. "It don't look natural to me."

"Nor to me," agreed Silver. "Messmates, if Flint was living, this would be a hot spot for us. Six they were, and six are we; and bones is what they are now."

"I saw Flint dead with my own eyes," said

Morgan. "Billy took me in. Flint was layin' there with pennies on his eyes."

"Sure enough he's gone to Hell," said the bandaged fellow; "but if ever a spirit walked about, it would be Flint's. He died bad, Flint did!"

"Aye, that he did," observed another. "He raged and hollered for rum, and sang 'Fifteen Men,' and I never liked to hear it since. It was hot in Savannah, and I heared in his voice he was dyin'."

"Come, stow this talk," said Silver. "He's dead, and he don't walk—leastways not by day. Don't mind Flint. The treasure waits on us."

We started forward, but the pirates now kept side by side, speaking in hushes. The terror of the dead Captain Flint had fallen on their spirits.

CHAPTER 32

THE TREASURE HUNT—
THE VOICE AMONG THE TREES

We all sat down to rest as soon as we reached the plateau. The men's morale had fallen. Silver and the sick men were tired.

The plateau's westward tilt gave us a wide view. Before us was the Cape of the Woods; behind us were the anchorage, Skeleton Island, and the open sea. The Spyglass rose sheer above us with its cliffs and single pines. The only sounds were the distant breakers and the chirps of insects.

Silver was taking bearings with his compass.

"There are three tall trees," said he, "about in the right line from Skeleton Island. 'Spyglass shoulder' must mean that lower point there. This is child's play—I've half a mind to eat first."

"I don't feel good," growled Morgan. "Thinkin' o' Flint done me in."

"Ah, Tom, praise your stars he's dead," said Silver.

"He were an ugly devil," cried a third pirate, shuddering, "all blue in the face!"

"That was the rum," added Merry. "It turned him blue, right enough."

Since finding the skeleton, their voices had dropped until they were now almost whispering. All of a sudden, from the trees in front of us, came a thin, trembling voice:

"Fifteen men on the dead man's chest—
Yo-ho-ho, and a bottle of rum!"

Never have I seen such terror. They all went terribly pale. Some leaped to their feet, some clawed at others. Morgan groveled on the ground.

"It's Flint, by God!" cried Merry.

The song suddenly stopped, as though someone had clapped his hand over the singer's mouth. It did not frighten me, and I found my companions' reactions very strange.

"Come," said Silver, struggling to speak through gray lips. "This won't do. Hold your ground. This is a bad start. I can't name the voice, but someone flesh and blood is playing a trick— take my word on that."

His courage and color returned as he spoke. The others had begun to calm down a little when the same voice broke out again—not singing, but in a faint distant hail that echoed from the cliffs of the Spyglass.

"Darby M'Graw! Darby M'Graw!" it wailed, over and over again. Then it rose higher, swore heavily, and cried out: "Fetch aft the rum, Darby!"

The mutineers remained rooted to the ground, staring wide-eyed in silent dread until long after the sound died away.

"That does it!" gasped one. "Let's go."

"They was his last words," moaned Morgan, "his last words alive."

Dick had his Bible out and was praying loudly. Apparently he had been a godly man before falling in with criminals at sea.

Silver was unconquered, but I could hear his teeth chattering.

"Nobody in this here island ever heard of Darby," he muttered, "but us here." And then, making a great effort, he cried, "Shipmates, I'm here to get that treasure, and I'll not be beat by man or devil! I never was feared of Flint alive, and by the powers, I'll face him dead. There's seven hundred thousand pounds nearby here. When did a gentleman o' fortune ever abandon that much money because of a drunk old seaman with a blue face, alive or dead?"

His irreverent words had the opposite effect of what he wanted. "Be careful, John!" said Merry, warningly. "Don't you cross a spirit."

The rest were all too terrified to reply. They huddled close to John, who had overcome his own jitters and was once again sly Long John.

"Spirit? Well, maybe," he said. "But there's one thing not clear to me: the echo. No man ever saw a spirit cast a shadow, so how can a spirit's voice have an echo? That ain't natural."

This argument seemed weak enough to me, but these were superstitious men. To my great wonder, George Merry was quite relieved.

"Well, that's so," he said. "You've a head upon your shoulders, John, and no mistake. Mates, this here crew is off course. And come to think of it, it was only somewhat like Flint's voice. It was more like somebody else's, now—like—"

"By the powers, Ben Gunn!" roared Silver.

"Aye, so it were," cried Morgan, springing up. "Ben Gunn it were!"

"It don't make sense, do it, now?" asked Dick. "Ben Gunn's not here in the flesh any more'n Flint."

"Why, nobody pays much attention to Ben Gunn, dead or alive," cried Merry.

Both their color and courage were restored, and the men were soon chatting while keeping an ear out. When no further sounds came, they shouldered the tools and set forth again. Merry walked in front with Silver's compass to keep them on the proper line with Skeleton Island. He was right: dead or alive, nobody cared about Ben Gunn.

Dick alone still held his Bible, looking around fearfully as he went, but he got no sympathy. Silver even needled him.

"I told you," said he. "You spoiled your Bible.

If it ain't no good to swear by, do you suppose a spirit cares for it? Not much!" But Dick was not comforted, and I could tell his fever was worsening. The heat, exertion, and fear were taking a toll.

The walking was easy here, slightly downhill through sparse pines. We were going pretty much northwest, with the Spyglass on one hand and the western bay on the other. I had looked up at this place while I was tossing and trembling in the coracle.

We reached the first of the tall trees, and the bearings proved it the wrong one. The same happened with the second tree. The third rose nearly two hundred feet into the air above a clump of underbrush, with a red trunk the width of a small house. It was likely visible far out to sea, and was the sort of landmark often entered on sailing charts.

My companions were far less impressed with the tree than with the notion of the gold buried beneath it. Their eyes burned; their feet grew speedier and lighter; ahead was their ticket to the lazy, wealthy lives they had always wanted.

It was hard going for Silver, hobbling and grunting on his crutch. He cursed like a madman when the flies settled on his hot, shiny face. I was shaken and had a hard time keeping up. When I stumbled, Silver yanked furiously at the line while giving me deadly looks. I had no trouble reading his thoughts. With the gold near, he no longer cared about his promise to the doctor, nor the doctor's warning. Surely he would seize the treasure, find and board the *Hispaniola* under cover of night, cut every honest throat aboard her, and sail away laden with crimes and riches.

Dick had fallen behind, babbling both prayers and curses as his fever rose. I was haunted by the thought of the tragedy that plateau had seen. Here, the terrible Captain Flint—who had died blue-faced at Savannah, singing and shouting for drink—had murdered six companions by his own hand. I thought I could still hear their dying cries in this peaceful grove.

We were now at the edge of the woods. "All together, mates, all together!" shouted Merry; and broke into a run. Ten yards further, they all stopped, and a low cry arose.

Silver doubled his pace, digging in his crutch like a man possessed. The next moment he and I also came to a dead halt.

Before us was a large hole, with the sides fallen in and grass sprouted on the bottom. In it were a broken pick-handle and the ruined boards from some packing boxes. One of these had a word branded on it: *Walrus*. You may recall that as the name of Flint's ship.

There was nothing else.

The seven hundred thousand pounds were gone!

CHAPTER 33

THE FALL OF A CHIEFTAIN

The pirates were stunned, but Silver had obviously been preparing for this moment. Before the disappointment sank into the others' minds, he changed his plan.

"Jim," he whispered, "take that, and stand by for trouble." He passed me a double-barreled pistol and edged northward, to put the hole between the others and us. He looked at me and nodded, but not quite in a friendly way. In disgust I whispered: "So you've changed sides again."

He had no time to answer. The pirates leaped into the pit, shouting and cursing and digging with their fingers. Morgan found a single gold coin, and held it up while swearing dreadfully. It went from hand to hand for a quarter of a minute.

"One coin!" roared Merry, shaking it at Silver. "That's your seven hundred thousand pounds, is it? You're the man to follow, ain't you, you wooden-headed lubber!"

"Dig away, boys," said Silver with cool insolence. "You might find some iron bolts and such."

"Mates, do you hear that?" screamed Merry. "He knew it all along. You can see it in his face."

"Ah, Merry," remarked Silver, "running for cap'n again? You're ambitious, to be sure."

But this time everyone was on Merry's side. They scrambled out of the hole with furious looks—luckily, on the opposite side from us, five against our two. Nobody was ready to strike first. Silver was as calm as I ever saw him. He may have been a criminal, but he was a brave man.

At last Merry spoke. "Mates, there's only two of them: the old cripple that blundered away our money, and that boy who's ruined everything. Now, mates—"

He raised his arm as if about to lead a charge. Just then—*crack! crack! crack!*—three musket-shots flashed from the nearby woods. Merry tumbled headfirst into the hole; the bandaged man spun around and fell on his side, dead but twitching. The other three turned and ran for it.

Long John quickly fired two pistol shots into the struggling Merry. As the stricken man looked up in his final agony, Long John said, "Well, George, I reckon I settled you."

Dr. Livesey, Gray, and Ben Gunn came out of the nutmeg trees, muskets smoking. "Forward!"

cried the doctor. "Be quick, my lads. We must reach the boats first." We set off at full speed.

How anxious Silver was to keep up with us! With his crutch, he had harder work than any able-bodied man. The doctor is still surprised his heart did not burst. By the time we reached the edge of the slope, he was already thirty yards behind us and completely winded.

"Doctor," he hailed, "see there! No hurry!"

Sure enough, we could see the three survivors running toward Mizzenmast Hill. They were heading the wrong way. We were already between them and the boats, so we sat down to rest while Long John caught up.

"Thank ye kindly, Doctor," says he, mopping his face. "You came just in time for me and Hawkins. It's you, Ben Gunn!" he added. "You look a fine sight, to be sure."

"I'm Ben Gunn, I am," replied the marooned man, wriggling in embarrassment. After a long pause he added, "How do, Mr. Silver? Pretty well, I thank ye, says you."

"Ben, Ben," murmured Silver, "to think what you've done to me!"

The doctor sent Gray back to bring one of the mutineers' abandoned pickaxes. When he returned, we proceeded downhill without hurry while Dr. Livesey filled in the story. Silver listened with great interest. Ben Gunn, considered a buffoon by his shipmates, was the hero from beginning to end.

Ben had found the skeleton while wandering the island. He had followed it to the large tree, found and dug up the treasure. The broken pick left in the hole was his. With many weary trips, he had hauled it all to a cave on the northeast coast, finishing up two months before the *Hispaniola* arrived. This cave, set into the two-peaked hill, also held a large supply of salted goat meat.

The doctor had coaxed this secret from him the afternoon of the stockade attack. Next morning, the doctor awoke and saw the *Hispaniola* gone, so he went to bargain with Silver. Neither the map nor the ship's supplies were needed, so Dr. Livesey offered these to Silver to buy time. If the loyal side could reach the cave without interference, they could easily guard the money while avoiding fever.

"As for you, Jim," he said, "I had to do my best for the loyal men. Can you blame me for thinking you disloyal?" I could not. I kept quiet as he continued.

"I knew that the mutineers would be very disappointed, Jim, and that you were in danger. I ran all the way to the cave. I left the squire to take care of the captain, and took Gray and Ben Gunn across the island to lay in wait. When I saw that Silver's men had a head start, and that Ben was faster than us, I sent him ahead to delay your group. He cleverly played on his old shipmates' superstitions. Thanks to Ben, the three of us were already hidden in ambush when the treasure hunters arrived."

"Ah," said Silver, "it were fortunate for me that I had Hawkins here. Were he not, doctor, you would have let them cut old John to bits."

"Without hesitation," replied Dr. Livesey cheerily.

We soon reached the boats. The doctor demolished one of them with the pickaxe, and we all boarded the other to row the eight or nine miles to North Inlet. We were soon skimming swiftly out of the straits. We rounded the southeast corner of the island, where we had towed the *Hispaniola* four days ago.

As we passed the two-pointed hill, we could see a figure against the black mouth of Ben Gunn's cave. It was the squire. We waved a handkerchief and gave him three cheers, Silver's voice joining in as heartily as the rest.

Three miles farther, just inside the mouth of North Inlet, we discovered the drifting *Hispaniola*. The last tide had lifted her off the beach. If there had been much wind or a strong tide current, she would have been lost or wrecked. As it was, she was in good condition except for the damage I had done to the mainsail. We boarded her, rigged another anchor, and dropped it in nine feet of water. We then rowed back around to Rum Cove, the nearest point to Ben Gunn's treasure-cave. Gray rowed back to the *Hispaniola* alone, to stand guard over her that night.

We climbed the gentle slope from the beach to the cave. The squire met us at the top. He spoke kindly to me, neither blaming nor praising my recent actions. Silver's courteous salute brought a very different reaction.

"John Silver," he said, red-faced, "you're a villain and a monstrous imposter, sir. I am asked not to prosecute you. Very well; I will not—but dead men hang upon your soul like millstones."

"Thank you kindly, sir," replied Long John, saluting again.

"Don't you dare thank me!" cried the squire. "Sparing you is a gross dereliction of my duty. Stand back."

We all entered the large, airy cave, which had a little spring and a pool of clear water. Captain Smollett lay near a big fire. In a far corner I could see great heaps of coins and stacks of gold bars: Flint's treasure, which had already cost seventeen lives from the *Hispaniola*. How many had died gathering it, what blood and sorrow, what good ships lost at sea, what cannon shots and shame and lies and cruelty, perhaps no living man could tell. Yet there were still three upon that island—Silver, old Morgan, and Ben Gunn—who had helped in these crimes, and hoped in vain to share in the reward.

"Come in, Jim," said the captain. "You're a good boy, but I don't think you and me'll go to sea again. Is that you, John Silver? What brings you here, man?"

"Returning to my duty, sir," answered Silver.

"Ah!" said the captain, and that was all.

I had a joyful supper that night with all my friends around me. Ben Gunn's salted goat made a fine meal, along with some delicacies and a bottle of old wine from the *Hispaniola*. Silver sat back almost out of the firelight. He ate heartily, leaped up eagerly when anyone wanted anything, and even joined quietly in our laughter. He was again the bland, helpful seaman he had been to start with.

CHAPTER 34

AND LAST

The next morning we got an early start hauling the great mass of gold. Each man could carry only two bars the mile down to the beach. Gray and Ben Gunn made many weary trips between the beach and the *Hispaniola* with as much as their boat could hold. The three surviving mutineers had probably had enough of fighting, but we posted a sentry on the hill just in case. Every day we stowed a new fortune aboard, with another fortune to stow tomorrow.

My task was to pack loose coins into breadbags. The coinage was even more interesting and diverse than Billy Bones's hoard: English, French, Spanish, Portuguese, and others. I saw the pictures of all the kings of Europe for the last hundred years. There were strange Oriental pieces with odd markings like spider webs. There were round coins, square coins, and coins with holes in the middle.

Silver was allowed complete freedom, but treated mostly with contempt. He seemed immune. He behaved as a friendly, loyal servant, always trying to be in favor, patient with our coldness. Ben Gunn shrunk away from his old quartermaster in terror. I had reason to think even less of him than the others did. After all, I had seen his treachery first hand as he repeatedly shifted loyalty from one side to the other to save his own skin. At the same time, I alone had something to thank him for. He had saved my life when I was his prisoner in the stockade. As a result, I was not as harsh with him as the others were.

As for those others, at first we heard nothing. On the third night, the doctor and I were strolling on the hill when we heard a strange, brief shrieking or singing noise from the thick darkness below.

"Heaven forgive them," said the doctor. "It's the mutineers!"

"All drunk, sir," added Silver from behind us.

"Drunk or raving," answered the doctor gruffly.

"Right you were, sir," replied Silver. "Hard to tell from up here."

"I can hardly ask you to understand a humane mind," returned the doctor with a sneer, "so my feelings may surprise you, Master Silver. If I were sure they were raving with fever—as I strongly suspect one is—I would leave this camp to help them despite the risk."

"Asking your pardon, sir, you would be very wrong," replied Silver. "You would lose your life, take my word on that. I'm on your side now, all the way, and I would not wish to see any of us hurt—you least of all, knowing the thanks I owes you. But these men down there, they'd betray you. They couldn't imagine you'd keep your word."

"I suppose not," said the doctor. "If anyone ought to be an expert in betrayal, it is our Master Silver."

That was nearly our last news of the three pirates. Another time we heard a faraway gunshot, then nothing more.

When we had all the gold bars and coin aboard, we loaded fresh water and goat meat until nightfall. Tomorrow we would set sail for home.

That night we held a council to determine the mutineers' fate. We agreed that we could not risk bringing them. We would have to maroon them, much to Ben Gunn's glee and Gray's strong approval. We left a good stock of powder and shot, most of the salted goat, a few medicines, and some other supplies and tools. The doctor added a handsome present of tobacco.

The next morning we rowed out to the *Hispaniola*. It took every man, and one boy, to hoist the anchor and set sail. We set a course out of North Inlet with the captain's flag from the stockade flapping at our mast.

The mutineers must have been watching us closer than we thought. We had to pass near the southern point of the narrows, and there we saw them. They were kneeling on the sand, arms upraised, pleading with us not to maroon them. I think it tore at all our hearts, but if we took them home, they must travel in irons and were destined for the gallows—an act of debatable kindness. The doctor hailed them and told them where to find the supplies. They continued to call us by name, begging us in God's name not to leave them to die.

At last, the ship began to draw out of earshot. One of them cried out, leaped to his feet, brought his musket to his shoulder and fired. The shot whistled over Silver's head and through the mainsail, and we took cover. When I looked out again they had disappeared from the beach, which was itself receding from sight. Before noon, to my joy, the highest rock of Treasure Island had sunk beyond the horizon.

We were so short of men that everyone on board had to work. The captain issued orders from a mattress in the stern. He was on the mend, but still had to rest. We could not risk the voyage home with such a skeleton crew. Between baffling winds and a couple of gales, we were all worn out by the time we landed in Spanish America.

We dropped anchor just at sundown in a beautiful land-locked gulf. The *Hispaniola* was immediately surrounded by shore-boats full of local inhabitants selling fruits and vegetables. The sight of so many good-humored faces, the delicious tropical fruits, and above all the lights of the town made a charming contrast to our dark, bloody adventure on the island. The doctor and the squire took me ashore, where we met the captain of an English warship. He invited us on board his vessel, where we had such an agreeable time that we did not return to the *Hispaniola* until daybreak.

Ben Gunn was on deck alone, and he began to squirm as soon as we came aboard. He soon confessed that he had let Silver escape. Ben assured us that he had done it to save our lives, which he said would have been lost if "that man with the one leg had stayed aboard."

The sea cook had also helped himself to a sack of coin worth perhaps six or seven hundred pounds, to help him on his further wanderings. Who knew what threats, false promises, and wheedling Silver had used on Ben? Indeed, who cared? I think we were all pleased to be so cheaply rid of him.

To make a long story short, we hired a few new hands and made a good cruise home. The *Hispaniola* reached Bristol just as Mr. Blandly was thinking of sending her sister-ship for us. Only five of the *Hispaniola*'s original crew returned with her. As our crew used to sing, "Drink and the devil had done for the rest." It was true enough. But at least we were not quite as depleted as that other ship they sang about:

> "With one man of her crew alive,
> What put to sea with seventy-five."

We all received handsome shares of the treasure, and each used it wisely or foolishly according to his nature. Captain Smollett is now retired from the sea. Gray was thrifty, and he is now mate and part owner of a fine full-rigged ship. Ben Gunn got a thousand pounds, which he spent or lost in less than three weeks and was back to begging. Dr. Livesey arranged him a job as groundskeeper. He is a great favorite with the country boys, though they laugh at his habit of talking to himself. And he sings in the church choir.

Of Silver, thank God, we have heard no more. I suspect he met up with his wife, and perhaps still lives in comfort with her and Captain Flint. He had best hope so, for his chances of comfort in the next world are very small.

The bar silver and weapons still lie, for all that I know, where Flint buried them. And I am content to leave them so. Oxen could not drag me back to Treasure Island. Even now, I sometimes awaken at night with the sharp voice of Captain Flint still ringing in my ears: "Pieces of eight! Pieces of eight!"

TREASURE ISLAND

AFTERWORD

ABOUT THE AUTHOR

From birth until the age of thirty-three, Robert Louis Stevenson repeatedly disappointed his parents. Although he often went against their wishes, they never failed to encourage their only child. Because of their patience and love during the first thirty-three years of his life, Stevenson was able to become a successful writer during the final eleven years of his life.

Robert Louis Stevenson was born on November 13, 1850 in Edinburgh, Scotland. From the time of his birth, he was a sickly child. His frail health was a worry to his parents, Thomas and Margaret. They hired a woman named Alison Cunningham to be his nurse. Cunningham became a part of the family for much of Stevenson's childhood. In addition to caring for the boy, she entertained him by telling or reading him stories. Some of these were Bible stories. Others were gruesome tales of Scottish religious martyrs. Still others were stories she read to him from serial novels. (Serial novels are novels printed in weekly or monthly installments.) Before long, Stevenson began writing stories himself. Some of these were retellings of Bible stories. His loving mother was an encouraging audience for his work. When Stevenson was sixteen, his parents published one of his pieces of writing as a pamphlet titled "The Pentland Rising." In it, Stevenson wrote about the murder of a group of Scotsmen who had rebelled against religious persecution. It was not, however, his parents' intention to encourage Stevenson to become a writer.

Stevenson's father and grandfather were engineers. The family assumed that the boy would join the family engineering firm once he completed his university degree. Initially, all seemed to be going according to plan. At seventeen, Stevenson enrolled in Edinburgh University to study engineering.

He showed promise in the field of engineering. In March of 1871, he presented a scientific paper to the Royal Scottish Society of Arts. He was awarded the society's Silver Medal for this work. Two weeks later, however, the twenty-year-old told his father that he intended to become a writer, rather than follow the family profession of engineering. This news was a disappointment and a worry to Thomas Stevenson. The disappointment was that his son would not follow the family tradition. The worry was that the young man wanted to go into a field that did not seem to be a suitable way to earn a living. Thomas Stevenson insisted that, if the young man would not become an engineer, he must study law. Stevenson agreed to do so.

Three years later, Stevenson disappointed his parents in a different way. His parents were religious people and Stevenson seemed to have strong religious beliefs as well. But then his father came across some papers that indicated that the young man had become an atheist, or one who does not believe in God. The shock drove a wedge between the young man and his parents. Stevenson himself felt terrible about this falling out. As he wrote to a friend, he saw himself as a "damned curse" on his family. After a time, however, his parents came to accept their son in spite of his attitude toward religion.

Throughout his eight years of university study, first in engineering and then in law, Stevenson continued to be a worry to his parents. He did enough work to pass his courses, but he preferred to spend his time on other activities. One of these was to teach himself to be a writer by imitating the styles of famous authors. Another was to wander around the older parts of Edinburg, becoming familiar with the inhabitants of the rough neighborhoods. During vacations, he traveled in France to meet young writers and painters. His parents were concerned about his health and about the company he was keeping.

In 1875 Stevenson received his law degree. By now he was sure he wanted to become a writer. As a result, he never did practice law, once again disappointing his parents. For the four years after he received his law degree, Stevenson spent much of his time traveling in Europe. During this period he wrote some short stories, some of which were published in magazines. He also wrote accounts of his travels. Stevenson's lack of income and his unfocused and unhealthy lifestyle were ongoing concerns to his parents. Before long, he gave them something more specific to worry about.

In the summer of 1876, he traveled to an artists' colony in France. There he became interested in an American woman named Fanny Osbourne. By the time she returned to America two years later, Stevenson was deeply in love with her. This relationship distressed his parents for four reasons. First, Fanny was an independent-minded "new woman." Second, she was eleven years older than their son. Third, she had a husband in California. And fourth, she had two children.

In August of 1879, Stevenson received a telegram from Fanny. (Neither of them ever revealed what the message said.) Without telling his parents in advance, he boarded a ship and sailed to America. Stevenson arrived in New York very ill and with very little money. He took a train to California and almost died during the journey. For the next several months he continued to be extremely ill. He was also emotionally upset because he was not certain if Fanny would get a divorce from her husband. When his parents learned what bad financial, physical, and mental shape he was in, they sent him enough money to keep him out of poverty.

Fanny and her husband finally divorced. On May 19, 1880, she and Stevenson were married. By August, he was well enough that the couple was able to travel to Scotland. Once Thomas and Margaret met Fanny, they quickly came to appreciate what a good influence she was on their son. She was able to keep after him about his health in a way that they had not been able to. For example, Stevenson had been in the habit of staying up late with hard-drinking friends. But Fanny put an end to such activities. This caused some of Stevenson's friends to resent her, but it probably also helped keep him alive. She also took an interest in his writing and assisted him with it.

Stevenson, now twenty-nine years old, and Fanny, now forty, settled in Scotland. Although Thomas and Margaret were glad to have their son home, they continued to worry about his health and his ability to earn a living. Neither his physical condition nor his financial situation improved over the next three years.

The summer of 1881 was a turning point in Stevenson's career. One rainy day, he and his twelve-year-old stepson (one of Fanny's children) were amusing themselves by drawing a map of an imaginary "Treasure Island." The map sparked Stevenson's imagination and he began to write a story based on it. The result was the book *Treasure Island*. It was published in 1883 and marked the beginning of Stevenson's popular and financial success. Over the next three years he wrote four of his most popular books—*A Child's Garden of Verses*, *The Black Arrow*, *The Strange Case of Dr. Jekyll and Mr. Hyde*, and *Kidnapped*—along with several other works.

His parents' patience and loving forgiveness had paid off. Finally, their son had settled into a lifestyle more appropriate to his fragile health. And finally, at the age of thirty-three, Robert Louis Stevenson found success.

Then, in the spring of 1887, Thomas Stevenson died. This was a serious blow to the popular author. That fall, Stevenson and Fanny moved to Saranac Lake, New York. While they were there, one of Stevenson's close friends back in Scotland accused Fanny of stealing a story from one of Stevenson's cousins. The accusation was false, but the friend never admitted he had done anything wrong in making the false charge. These two events—the death of his father and betrayal by a close friend—greatly upset Stevenson. After a period of depression over these events, he reached another turning point in his life.

In 1888, Stevenson and his family struck out

for a new life. He rented a yacht and took his family, including his widowed mother, on a cruise of the South Pacific. He hoped the cruise would help him heal emotionally and physically. After several months of stopping at various islands for brief periods of time, they landed in the Samoan Islands. They settled there and built a house where they lived until Stevenson's death.

During his years traveling and living in the South Pacific, Stevenson continued to write. He loved the diverse peoples of the islands and he hated the exploitation of the inhabitants by the European colonial rulers and traders. Some of his writing was devoted to these views. He became a hero to the original inhabitants of the islands. His forcefully stated views did not, however, win him any friends among the colonial administrators. But he was too popular an author for them to dare to try to silence him.

Much as he loved the South Pacific, he also greatly missed Scotland. The thought that he would never see his homeland again weighed on him. As he wrote to one friend, "I shall never set my foot again upon the heather. Here I am until I die, and here will I be buried. The word is out and the doom written." Many critics feel that, although his writings from his years in the South Pacific are not his most famous, they are his best work. He died of a stroke in 1894 in his house at Vailima, Samoa. He was forty-four years old.

ABOUT THE BOOK

Robert Louis Stevenson's *Treasure Island* was published in 1883. Since then, the book has never been out of print. What makes the novel continue to be so popular more than 120 years after it was written? There are several answers to this question.

First, there is exciting action. In Chapter 1, Billy Bones pulls a knife on Dr. Livesey and a tense standoff follows. In Chapter 2, Bones slashes Black Dog with his cutlass and drives him from the inn. In Chapter 3, Bones receives a death threat, then collapses and dies from a massive stroke. Almost every chapter in the book has at least one action scene. But action alone is not enough to keep a book popular for 120 years.

Second, Stevenson sets up situations that raise questions in the reader's mind. The reader keeps reading to find the answers. On the first page, a menacing, scarred-faced sailor shows up at the Admiral Benbow Inn. Who is this man who calls himself Captain? Why is he afraid of other sailors? Who is the "seafaring man with one leg" that he especially fears? The only way to find out is to keep reading. But as we keep reading, new questions crop up. Why is Black Dog in Long John Silver's tavern? Is it just coincidence that Silver has named his tavern the Sign of the Spyglass and the map of Treasure Island refers to Spyglass Hill? Why do all of the sailors that the squire has hired seem to know all the details of the "secret" voyage they are going on? Why does the first mate disappear over-board one dark night? Why do Dr. Livesey and the others abandon the blockhouse to Long John Silver and the mutineers? Why does the Doctor give Long John Silver the map that shows where the treasure is buried? Whose side is Long John Silver on? Eventually, all of the questions are answered. But sometimes, we have to piece the answers together for ourselves from evidence Stevenson reveals bit by bit.

A third important element in the continuing popularity of *Treasure Island* is the depth of the characters. This can most easily be seen in Jim Hawkins. Jim is important because he is the narra-tor, the one who tells us the story. But what really makes him important is that he is a dynamic char-acter—a character that changes over the course of the novel.

One way in which Jim changes is that he goes from being a boy who acts impulsively to a young man who plans his actions. In Chapter 13, when Jim decides to sneak ashore on Treasure Island, he hides on one of the boats going ashore. Almost immediately Jim says, "I began to regret my impulse." He soon realizes he has gotten himself into a perilous situation. He tells us, "I considered myself doomed. . . . There was nothing left for me but death—either by starvation or at the hands of the mutineers." Only his lucky encounter with Ben Gunn saves him. In Chapter 22, on the other hand, Jim makes plans before he sneaks out of the stockade. Before leaving, he fills his pockets with biscuits so that he will have food in case "anything bad should happen." And he arms himself with two pistols. And he has a purpose: "I planned to go down to the white rock and see if Ben Gunn's boat was there." When he realizes that the mutineers are likely to sail off in the *Hispaniola*, leaving Jim and his friends on the island with no means of escape, he further develops his plan in order to stop the pirates. Not only has he become capable of planning ahead; he is also able to adapt and adjust his plan as the circumstances evolve. This is a significant change in Jim.

A second way that Jim changes and grows is in his reaction to his own instincts. In Chapter 8, when Jim first sees Long John Silver, he says that "this clean, pleasant landlord did not resemble those desperate men" like Black Dog or Pew. But his instinct warns him to be careful of this man. He tells us that the sight of Black Dog drinking in Silver's tavern "had made me suspicious." In spite of this internal alarm, Jim is won over by Silver's charming manner. A few minutes later, Jim tells us that, "I began to think him a great shipmate." In Chapter 10, Jim's instinct gives him another warning. As the *Hispaniola* sets sail, Silver begins to sing the same song Billy Bones always sang. Jim's gut warns him, for he tells us that he "could almost hear the voice of the captain [Billy Bones] joining in the chorus." But Jim ignores this warning sign. Instead, he falls for Silver's flattering words and compliments. Only later, after he sees clear evidence, does Jim realize how truly dangerous the man is. By contrast, in Chapter 15, Jim does follow his instincts. When he first meets Ben Gunn, Jim does not make a decision based on the man's appearance. The man seems childlike and strange. He says crazy things about dreaming of cheese and making Jim rich. In spite of Gunn's seeming to be a madman, Jim makes "an impulsive decision to trust him." He listens to his instincts— and he is right. Trusting this man is an important step in saving Jim's own life and the lives of his friends.

A third way that Jim changes is in his ability to overcome his fear of evil and stand up for himself. In Chapter 11, Jim, while hiding in the apple barrel, overhears Long John Silver's mutiny plans. Once he begins to realize what a truly dangerous man Silver is, he finds it hard to face him. In Jim's words, "When I saw [Silver] drawing near me, I wanted to shudder." However, by Chapter 28, Jim is ready to face up to this manipulative and threatening man. Jim is Silver's prisoner in the blockhouse. The pirate tells Jim he would welcome the boy into the company of mutineers. But Jim realizes that, if he does not agree, he will be killed. As Jim says, ". . . I could feel the threat of death hanging over me." Instead of shuddering in horror, Jim takes Silver on and beats the man at his own game. He tells the pirate, ". . . all your plans are in shambles—ship lost, treasure lost, men lost, your whole business wrecked—and *I* did it!" Jim then explains in detail how he overheard the mutiny plot, revealed it to Dr. Livesey and the others, and stole the schooner and hid it, killing Israel Hands in the process. Finally, he convinces Silver that there is a good reason for the pirate to spare his life:

> I have the last laugh, and I do not fear you. Kill me or spare me. I don't care. But I'll say one thing: if you spare me, bygones are bygones, and when you fellows are in court for piracy, I'll help you if I can. Now *you* choose. Kill another and do yourselves no good, or spare me and keep a witness to save you from the gallows.

Instead of cowering, Jim has the courage to face an incredibly powerful enemy and bargain for his life.

But there is one quality Jim has that does not change during the novel. It is his compassion. In Chapter 3, when Billy Bones dies, Jim tells us, "My reaction still surprises me, for I had never liked him, though I had begun to pity him. As soon as I saw that he was dead, I burst into a flood of tears." And he continues to be compassionate right through the final chapter of the book. In spite of Silver's readiness to kill Jim if it would help improve Silver's situation, Jim recognizes that Silver has also saved him. In the final chapter Jim says:

> I had reason to think even less of [Silver] than the others did. After all, I had seen his treachery first hand as he repeatedly shifted loyalty from one side to the other to save his own skin. At the same time, I alone had something to thank him for. He had saved my life when I was his prisoner in the stockade. As a result, I was not as harsh with him as the others were.

He sees the worst in the man—he has seen Silver kill a man in cold blood. But he also acknowledges something worthwhile about Silver—the fact that Silver spared Jim's life when the other mutineers would have killed the boy.

There are many elements that make *Treasure Island* continue to be popular. The action and the intriguing questions are certainly important. They make the book interesting. But most important of all is Jim's dynamic character. This dynamic character teaches four lessons that are as important today as they were 120 years ago: think before you act; trust your own instincts; act courageously in the face of evil; and be compassionate.

If you liked
Treasure Island,
you might be interested in other
books in the Townsend Library.

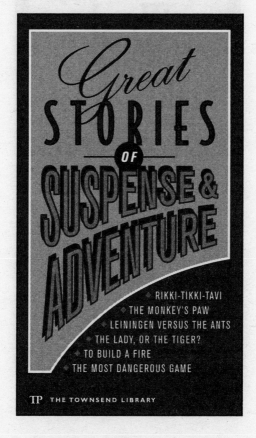

continued on following pages

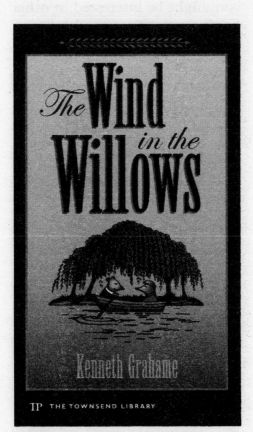

The Wind in the Willows

Kenneth Grahame

TP THE TOWNSEND LIBRARY

JACK LONDON

White Fang

TP THE TOWNSEND LIBRARY

THE ADVENTURES OF
TOM SAWYER
MARK TWAIN
TP THE TOWNSEND LIBRARY

MARK TWAIN

The Prince AND The Pauper

THE JUNGLE BOOK

RUDYARD KIPLING

THE TOWNSEND LIBRARY TP

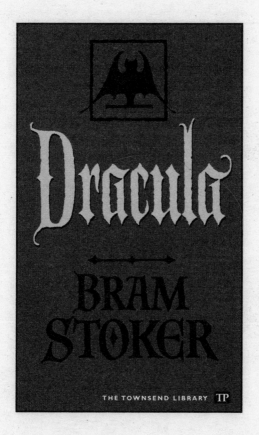

THE TOWNSEND LIBRARY TP

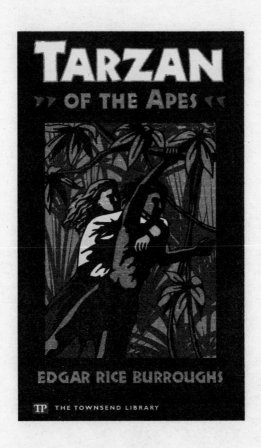

**For more information, visit us at
www.townsendpress.com**